TYCOON'S FORBIDDEN CINDERELLA

TYCOON'S FORBIDDEN CINDERELLA

MELANIE MILBURNE

MILLS & BOON

First published in Great Britain 2018
by Mills & Boon, an imprint of HarperCollins*Publishers*
1 London Bridge Street, London, SE1 9GF

Large Print edition 2018

ISBN: 978-0-263-07433-8

MIX
Paper from
responsible sources
FSC® C007454

This book is produced from independently certified FSC™ paper to ensure responsible forest management. For more information visit www.harpercollins.co.uk/green.

Printed and bound in Great Britain
by CPI Group (UK) Ltd, Croydon, CR0 4YY

To my dear friend Julie Greenwood.

We have been friends since the
seventh grade and I can't imagine how
different life would be if I hadn't met you.

I have so many fun memories of us horse
riding, and sitting in the mulberry tree
at my parents' farm with purple-stained
fingers and mouths.

You are one of a kind.

Love always. Xxxx

CHAPTER ONE

AUDREY EYED HER mother's wedding invitation as if it were a cockroach next to her breakfast teacup and toast plate. 'I would do anything to get out of this wedding party and I mean *anything*.'

Rosie, her flatmate, slipped into the seat opposite and pinched a slice of toast off Audrey's plate and began munching. 'Three times a bridesmaid, huh? Go you.'

Audrey sighed. 'Yes, well, being a bridesmaid three times would be bad enough but they're my mother's marriages and all to Harlan Fox. I thought she'd learned her lesson by now.'

'I guess that does complicate things a bit…' Rosie twisted her mouth in a *glad-it's-you-and-not-me* manner.

'I don't know why my mother hasn't learnt

from her past two mistakes.' Audrey stirred her tea until it created a whirlpool similar to the one she was feeling in her stomach. 'Who marries the same man *three* times? I can't bear another one of my mother's marriages. I can't bear another one of my mother's divorces. None of them were civilised and private. They were nasty and horribly public.' Her teaspoon fell against the saucer with a clatter. 'That's the problem with having a soap opera star for a parent. Nothing they do ever escapes public attention. Nothing. Good or bad or just plain dead embarrassing, it's all splashed over the gossip magazines and the net for millions to read.'

'Yeah, I kind of figured that after that spread about your mother's affair with one of the young cameramen on set,' Rosie said. 'Amazing she has a daughter of twenty-five and yet she can still pull guys like a barman pulls beers.'

'Yes, well, if that wasn't bad enough, Harlan Fox is even more famous than my mother.' Audrey frowned and pushed her cup and saucer away as if it had mortally offended her. 'What can she possibly see in an aging rock star of a heavy metal band?'

'Maybe it's because Harlan and his band mates are in the process of reforming to go back on the tour?' Rosie had clearly been reading the gossip pages rather avidly.

Audrey rolled her eyes. 'A process somewhat stalled by the fact that two of its members are still in rehab for drug and alcohol issues.'

Rosie licked a droplet of raspberry jam off her finger and asked, 'Is Harlan's hot-looking son Lucien going to be best man again?'

Audrey sprang up from the table as if her chair had suddenly exploded. The mere mention of Lucien Fox's name was enough to make her grind her teeth until her molars rolled over and begged for mercy. She scooped her teacup off the table and poured the contents in the sink, wishing she were throwing it in Lucien's impossibly handsome face. 'Yes.' She spat out the word like a lemon pip.

'Funny how you two have never hit it off,' Rosie said. 'I mean, you'd think you'd have heaps in common. You've both lived in the shadow of a celebrity parent. And you've been step-siblings on and off for the last…how long's it been now?'

Audrey turned from the sink and gripped the back of the chair. 'Six years. But it's not going to happen again. No way. This wedding is *not* going to go ahead.'

Rosie's eyebrows lifted until they met her fringe. 'What? You think you can talk them out of it?'

Audrey released her stranglehold on the chair and picked up her phone from the table and checked for messages. Still no answer from her mother. Damn it. 'I'm going to track Mum and Harlan down and give them a stern talking-to. I'll resort to blackmail if I have to. I have to stop them marrying. I *have* to.'

Rosie frowned. 'Track them down? Why? Have they gone into hiding or something?'

'They've both turned off their phones. Their publicists apparently have no idea where they've gone.'

'But you do?'

She drummed her fingers on the back of her phone. 'No, but I have a hunch and I'm going to start there.'

'Have you asked Lucien where he thinks they might be or are you still not talking since the last divorce? How many years ago was that again?' Rosie asked.

'Three,' Audrey said. 'For the last six years my mother and Harlan have been hooking up, getting hitched and then divorcing in a hate fest that makes headlines around the world. I'm over it. I'm not going to let it happen again. They can hook up if they want to but another marriage is out. O.U.T. Out.'

Rosie shifted her lips from side to side as if observing an unusual creature in captivity. 'Wow. You really have a thing about weddings, don't you? Don't you want to get married one day?'

'No. I do not.' Audrey knew she sounded like a starchy old spinster from a nineteenth-century novel but she was beyond caring. She hated weddings. Capital H hated them. She felt like throwing up when she saw a white dress. Maybe she wouldn't hate weddings so much if she hadn't been dragged to so many of her mother's. Before Harlan Fox, Sibella Merrington had had three husbands and not one of them had been Audrey's father. Audrey had no idea who her father was and apparently neither did her mother, although Sibella had narrowed it down to three men.

What was it with her mother and the number three?

'You didn't answer my question,' Rosie said. 'Are you talking to Lucien again or not?'

'Not.'

'Maybe you should reconsider,' Rosie said. 'You never know, he might prove to be an ally in your mission to stop his dad and your mum getting married.'

Audrey snorted. 'The day I speak again to that arrogant, stuck-up jerk will be the day hell turns into an ice factory.'

'Why do you hate him so much? What's he ever done to you?'

Audrey turned and snatched her coat off the hook behind the door and shrugged it on, pulling her hair out of the collar. She faced her flatmate. 'I don't want to talk about it. I just hate him, that's all.'

Rosie's brows shot up again like skyrockets and she leaned forward in her chair, eyes sparkling with intrigue. 'Did he try it on with you?'

Audrey's cheeks were suddenly feeling so hot she could have cooked another round of toast on them. No way was she going to confess it was *she* who had done the 'trying it on' and been rejected.

Mortifyingly, embarrassingly, ego-crushingly rejected.

Not once but two times. Once when she was eighteen and again when she was twenty-one, both times at her mother's wedding reception to his father. Another good reason to prevent such a marriage occurring again.

No more wedding receptions.

No more champagne.

No more gauche flirting with Lucien Fox.

Oh, God, why, why, *why* had she tried to kiss him? She had been planning to peck him on the cheek to show how sophisticated and cool she was about their respective parents getting married. But somehow her lips had moved. Or maybe his had moved. What did it matter whose had moved? Their mouths had almost touched. It was the closest a man's mouth had ever been to hers.

But he had jerked away as if she had poison on her lips.

The same thing happened at their parents' next wedding. Audrey had been determined to act as if nothing could faze her. She was going to act as if the previous almost-kiss had never happened. To show him it hadn't had any impact on her at all. But after a few champagnes to give her the courage to get on the dance floor, she'd breezed past Lucien and hadn't been able to stop herself from giving him a spontaneous little air kiss. Her mouth had aimed for the air between his cheek and hers but someone bumped her from behind and she had fallen against him.

She'd grabbed at the front of his shirt to stop herself from falling. He'd put his hands on her hips to steady her.

And for a moment…an infinitesimal moment when the noise of the reception faded away and it felt they were completely and utterly alone… she'd thought he was going to kiss her. So she'd…

Oh, God, she hated thinking about it even now...

She'd leaned up on tiptoe, closed her eyes and waited for him to kiss her. And waited. And waited.

But of course he hadn't.

Even though Audrey had been tipsy on both occasions, and a part of her knew Lucien had done the honourable thing by rejecting her clumsy advances, another part of her—the female, insecure part—wondered if any man would ever be attracted to her. Would any man ever want to kiss her, much less make love to her? She was twenty-five and still a virgin. She hadn't been on a date since she was a teenager.

Not that she hadn't been asked a few times but she'd always declined because she could never tell if guys wanted to go out with her for the right reason. Her first date at the age of sixteen had been a disaster—an ego-smashing disaster she would do anything to avoid repeating. She'd only been asked out because of who her mother was. It had nothing to do with *her* whether the boy liked her or not. It was about her celebrity mother.

It was *always* about her celebrity mother.

Audrey picked up her keys and the overnight bag she'd packed earlier. 'I'm heading out of town for the weekend.'

Rosie's eyes twinkled like they belonged on a Christmas tree. 'Am I allowed to know where you're going or is it a state secret?'

It wasn't that Audrey didn't trust her flatmate, but even Rosie with her down-to-earth nature could at times be a little star-struck by Audrey's mother. 'Sorry, Rosie. I have to keep the press out of this if I can. With Mum and Harlan in hiding, the first person the paps will come looking for is me.'

Please, God, not again. The press had followed her relentlessly after her mother had gone to ground. At Audrey's flat. She'd stayed for three weeks and had taken three overdoses, not serious enough for hospitalisation but serious enough for Audrey to want to prevent another marriage between her mother and the hard-partying Harlan Fox.

'What about Lucien?'

'What about Lucien?' Even saying his name made Audrey's spine tighten and her scalp prickle as if a thousand ants were tugging on the roots of her hair.

'What if Lucien wants to know where you are?'

'He won't. Anyway, he's got my number.'

Not that he'd ever used it in the last three years. Or the last six. But then, why would he? She was hardly his type. His type was tall and blonde and sophisticated, women who didn't drink too much champagne when they were feeling nervous or insecure and out of their depth.

'Gosh, how lucky are you to be on Lucien Fox's speed dial.' Rosie's expression had gone all dreamy. 'I wish I had his number. I don't suppose you'd—?'

Audrey shook her head. 'It'd be a waste of time if I did. He doesn't date boring homespun girls like us. He only dates size zero supermodels.'

Rosie sighed. 'Yeah, like that one he's been dating now for weeks and weeks—Viviana Prestonward.'

Something slipped in Audrey's stomach. 'H-has he?' Her voice came out scratchy and she cleared her throat. 'I mean, yes, yes, I know.'

'Viviana's amazingly beautiful.' Rosie's expression became one part wistful, three parts envious. 'I saw a picture of them at a charity ball last month. Everyone's saying they're about to become engaged. Some girls have all the luck. They get the best looks and the best guys.'

'I wouldn't call Lucien Fox a prize catch.' Audrey couldn't keep the bitter edge from her tone.

'He might be good-looking and rich but his personality needs a serious makeover. He's so stiff and formal you'd think he'd been potty-trained at gunpoint.'

Rosie tilted her head again in her studying-an-exotic-creature manner. 'Maybe he'll ask you to be the bridesmaid at his wedding too, I mean, since you're going to be step-siblings again.'

Audrey clenched her teeth hard enough to crack a coconut. 'Not if I can help it.'

Audrey drove out of London and within a couple of hours pulled into the country lane that led to the secluded cottage in the Cotswolds. Her mother had bought the house when she landed her first role on television. It often amazed Audrey that her mother hadn't sold it by now, but somehow the cottage remained even though several husbands and their houses had not.

It was too small to be the sort of place the press would expect to find Sibella and Harlan, so it was the first place on Audrey's list. Her mother had left a hint in the note on her doorstep, along with the invitation:

Gone to smell the daffodils with Harlan.

That could only mean Bramble Cottage. At this time of year the rambling garden was full of daffodils. Along the lane, in the fields, under the trees, along the bank of the stream—the swathes of yellow had always delighted Audrey.

Bramble Cottage was a perfect hideaway as it was on a long country lane lined with hedgerows and lots of overarching trees, creating a leafy tunnel. The lane had a rickety bridge over a trickling stream that occasionally swelled enough with rainwater to be considered a river.

When she came down to the cottage with her mother as a child, Audrey had been fascinated by the trees along the lane because they looked as if they were reaching down to hug her. Going through that shady green tunnel had been like driving into another world, a magical world where it was just her and her mother. A safe world. A world where there were no strange men coming and going from her mother's bedroom.

No press lurking about for candid shots of Sibella's painfully shy daughter.

Audrey couldn't see any sign of activity at the cottage when she got out of her car but she knew her mother and Harlan would have covered their tracks well. On closer inspection, however, she realised the cottage looked a little neglected. She'd thought there was a caretaker who kept an eye on things. There were often months and months or even a couple of years between her mother's fleeting visits. The garden was overgrown but in a way that was part of the charm of the place. Audrey loved how the plants spilled over the garden beds, their blooms filling the air with the fresh and hopeful fragrance of spring.

Audrey left her car parked in the shade of the biggest oak tree a short distance away so as to keep her car from being seen if any paparazzi happened to do a drive-by. She did a mental high-five when she saw the marks of recent tyre tracks on the pebbled area in front of the cottage. She bent down so she could inspect the tracks a little more closely. A car had come in and gone out again, which meant her mother and Harlan hopefully weren't far away. Probably picking up supplies or something. 'Or something' being copious amounts of alcohol most likely.

She straightened and glanced up at the suddenly darkening sky. That was another thing she loved about this place—watching a spring storm from the cosy shelter of the cottage. The spare key was under the left-hand plant pot but Audrey gave the door a quick knock just in case either her mother or Harlan was still inside. When there was no answer, she unlocked the door just as the rain started to pelt down as if someone had turned on a tap.

She closed the door and looked around the cottage but it didn't look as though anyone had been there in months. Disappointment sat on her chest like an overstuffed sofa. She'd been so certain she would find them here. Had she misread her mother's note?

She glanced at the cobwebs hanging from a lampshade and suppressed an icy shiver. There was a fine layer of dust over the furniture and the air inside the cottage had a musty, unaired smell. So much for the caretaker, then. But Audrey figured this would be a good test of the hideously expensive therapy she'd undergone to rid herself of her spider phobia. She pulled back the curtains to let more light in but the storm clouds had gathered to such an extent the world outside had a yellowish, greenish tinge that intensified with each flash of lightning. She turned on the sitting room light and it cast a homey glow over the deep, cushiony sofas and the wing chair positioned in front of the fireplace.

Audrey was battling with an acute sense of dismay that her mission to track down her mother and Harlan had come to a dead end and a sense of sheer unmitigated joy she had the cottage to herself during a storm. She figured she might as well stay for an hour or two to set the place in order, maybe even stay the night while she thought up a Plan B.

She reassured herself with the possibility that her mother and Harlan would return at any minute. After all, someone had been here—she'd seen the tyre marks. All she had to do was wait until they got back and sit them down and talk them out of this ridiculous third marriage.

Audrey glanced at the fireplace. Was it cold enough to light a fire? There was kindling and wood in the basket next to the fireplace, and before she could talk herself out of it she got to work setting a fire in the grate. It would come in handy if the power was to go off, which was not uncommon during a storm.

As if by her just thinking of a power cut, the light above her head flickered and a flash of lightning rent the sky outside. A sonic boom of thunder sounded, and it made even an avid storm-lover such as she jump. The light flickered again and then went out. It left the room in a low, ghostly sort of light that reminded her of the setting of a fright flick she'd watched recently. A shiver scuttled over her flesh like a legion of little furry feet.

It's just a storm. You love storms.

For once the self-talk wasn't helping. There was something about this storm that felt different. It was more intense, more ferocious.

Between the sound of the rain lashing against the windows and the crash of thunder, she heard another sound—car tyres spinning over the pebbled driveway.

Yes!

Her hunch had been spot-on. Her mother and Harlan were returning. Audrey jumped up to peep out of the window and her heart gave a carthorse kick against her breastbone.

No. No. No.

Not Lucien Fox. Why was he here?

She hid behind part of the curtain to watch him approach the front door, her breathing as laboured as the pair of antique bellows next to the fireplace. The rain was pelting down on his dark head but he seemed oblivious. Would he see her car parked under the oak tree?

She heard Lucien's firm knock on the door. Why hadn't she thought to lock it when she came into the cottage? The door opened and then closed.

Should she come out or hide here behind the curtain, hoping he wouldn't stay long enough to find her? The *Will I or won't I?* was like a see-saw inside her head.

He came into the sitting room and Audrey's heart kept time with the tread of his feet on the creaky floorboards.

Step-creak-boom-step-creak-boom-step-creak-boom.

'Harlan?' Lucien's deep baritone never failed to make her spine tingle. 'Sibella?'

Audrey knew it was too late to step out from her hiding place. She could only hope he would leave before he discovered her. How long was he going to take? Surely he could see no one had been here for months… *Yikes.* She forgot she had been laying a fire. Her breathing rate accelerated, her pulse pounding as loud as the thunder booming outside. She'd been about to strike the match when the power had gone off and it was now lying along with the box it came from on the floor in front of the fireplace.

Would he see it?

Another floorboard creaked and Audrey held her breath. But then her nose began to twitch from the dust clinging to the curtain. There was one thing she did not have and that was a ladylike sneeze. Her sneezes registered on the Richter scale. Her sneezes could trigger an earthquake in Ecuador. Her sneezes had been known to cause savage guard dogs to yelp and small babies to scream. She could feel it building, building, building… She pressed a finger under her nose as hard as she possibly could, her whole body trembling with the effort to keep the sinus explosion from happening.

A huge lightning flash suddenly zigzagged across the sky and an ear-splitting boom of thunder followed, making Audrey momentarily forget about controlling her sneeze. She clutched the curtain in shock, wondering if she'd been struck by lightning. Would she be found as a little pile of smoking ashes behind this curtain?

But clutching the curtain brought the dusty fabric even closer to her nostrils and the urge to sneeze became unbearable.

'Ah... Ah... Choo!'

It was like a bomb going off, propelling her forwards, still partially wrapped in the curtain, bringing the rail down with a clatter.

Even from under the dense and mummy-like shroud, Audrey heard Lucien's short, sharp expletive. Then his hands pulled at the curtain, finally uncovering her dishevelled form. 'What the hell?'

'Hi…' She sat up and gave him a fingertip wave.

He frowned at her. *'You?'*

'Yep, me.' Audrey scrambled to her feet with haste not grace, wishing she'd worn jeans instead of a dress. But jeans made her thighs look fat, she thought, so a dress it was. She smoothed down the cotton fabric over her thighs and then finger-combed her tousled hair. Was he comparing her with his glamorous girlfriend? No doubt Viviana could stumble out of a musty old curtain and still look perfect. Viviana probably had a tiny ladylike sneeze too. And Viviana probably looked amazing in jeans.

'What are you doing here?' His tone had that edge of disapproval that always annoyed her.

'Looking for my mum and your dad.'

Lucien's ink-black brows developed a mocking arch. 'Behind the curtain?'

Audrey gave him a look that would have withered tumbleweed. 'Funny, ha-ha. So what brings you here?'

He bundled up the curtain as if he needed something to do with his hands, his expression as brooding as the sky outside. 'Like you, I'm looking for my father and your mother.'

'Why did you think they'd come here?'

He put the roughly folded curtain over the back of the wing chair and then picked up the curtain rail, setting it to one side. 'My father sent me a text, mentioning something about a quiet weekend in the country.'

'Did his text say anything about daffodils?'

Lucien looked at her as if she'd mentioned fairies instead of flowers. 'Daffodils?'

Audrey folded her arms across her middle. 'Didn't you notice them outside? This place is Wordsworth's heaven.'

The corner of his mouth twitched into an almost-smile. But then his mouth went back to its firm and flat humourless line. 'I think we've been led on a wild-goose chase—or a wild-daffodil chase.'

This time it was Audrey who was trying not to smile. Who knew he had a sense of humour under that stern schoolmastery thing he had going on? 'I suppose you got the invitation to their wedding?'

His expression reminded her of someone not quite over a stomach bug. 'You too?'

'Me too.' She let out a sigh. 'I can't bear to be a bridesmaid for my mother again. Her taste in bridesmaid dresses is nearly as bad as her taste in men.'

If he was annoyed by her veiled slight against his father he didn't show it. 'We need to stop them from making another stupid mistake before it's too late.'

'We?'

His dark blue gaze collided with hers. Was it even possible to have eyes that shade of sapphire? And why did he have to have such thick, long eyelashes when she had to resort to lashings of mascara? 'Between us we must be able to narrow down the search. Where does your mother go when she wants to get away from the spotlight?'

Audrey rolled her eyes. 'She never wants to get away from the spotlight. Not now. In the early days she did. But it looks like she hasn't been here in months, possibly a year or more. Maybe even longer.'

Lucien ran a finger over the dusty surface of the nearest bookshelf, inspecting his fingertip like a forensics detective. He looked at her again. 'Can you think of anywhere else they might go?'

'Erm… Vegas?'

'I don't think so, not after the last time, remember?'

Audrey dearly wished she could forget. After her clumsy air kiss to Lucien—*as if that hadn't been bad enough*—her mother and his father had been ridiculously drunk at the reception of their second wedding and had got into a playful food fight. Some of the guests joined in and before long the room was trashed and three people were taken to hospital and four others arrested over a scuffle that involved a bowl of margarita punch and an ice bucket.

The gossip magazines ran with it for days and the hotel venue banned Harlan and Sibella from ever going there again. The fact that Audrey's mother had been the first to throw a profiterole meant that Lucien had always blamed Sibella and not his father. 'You're right. Not Vegas. Besides, they want us at the wedding to witness the ceremony. Not that the invitation mentioned where it was being held, just a date and venue to be advised.'

Lucien paced the floor, reminding her of a cougar in a cat carrier. 'Think. Think. Think.'

Audrey wasn't sure if he was speaking to her or to himself. The thing was, she found it difficult to think when he was around. His presence disturbed her too much. She couldn't stop herself studying his brooding features. He was one of the most attractive men she'd ever seen—possibly *the* most.

Tall and broad-shouldered and with a jaw you could land a fighter jet on. His mouth always made her think of long, sense-drugging kisses. Not that she'd had many of those, and certainly none from him, but it didn't stop her fantasising. He had thick, black, wavy hair that was neither long nor short but casually styled with the ends curling against his collar. He was clean-shaven but there was enough regrowth to make her wonder how it would feel to have that sexy stubble rub up against her softer skin.

Lucien stopped pacing and met her gaze and frowned. 'What?'

Audrey blinked. 'What?'

'I asked first.'

She licked her lips, which felt as dry as the dust on the bookshelves. 'I was just thinking. I always stare when I think.'

'What are you thinking?'

How hot you look in those jeans and that close-fitting cashmere sweater.

Audrey knew she was blushing, for she could feel her cheeks roaring enough to make lighting a fire pointless. She could have warmed the whole of England with the radiant heat coming off her face. Possibly half of Europe. 'I think the storm is getting worse.'

It was true. The lightning and thunder were much more intense and the rain had now turned into hail, landing like stones on the slate-tiled roof.

Lucien glanced out of the window and swore. 'We'll have to wait it out before we leave. It's too dangerous to drive down that lane in this weather.'

Audrey folded her arms across her middle again and raised her chin. 'I'm not leaving with you, so you can get that thought out of your head right now.'

His eyes took in her indomitable stance as if he were staring down at a small, recalcitrant child. 'I want you with me when we finally track them down. We need to show them we are both vehemently against this marriage.'

No way was she going on a tandem search with him. 'Were you listening?' She planted her feet as if she were conducting a body language workshop for mules. 'I said I'm not leaving. I'm going to stay the night and tidy this place up.'

'With no power on?'

Audrey had forgotten about the power cut. But even if she had to rub two sticks together to make a fire she would do it rather than go anywhere with him. 'I'll be fine. The fire will be enough. I'm only staying the one night.'

He continued to look at her as if he thought a white van and a straitjacket might be useful right about now. 'What about your thing with spiders?'

How like him to remind her of her embarrassing childhood phobia. But she had no reason to be ashamed these days. She'd taken control. Ridiculously expensive control. Twenty-eight sessions with a therapist that had cost more than her car. She would have done thirty sessions but she'd run out of money. Her income as a library archivist only went so far. 'I've had therapy. I'm cool with spiders now. Spiders and me, we're like that.' She linked two of her fingers in a tight hug.

His expression looked as though he belonged as keynote speaker at a sceptics' conference. 'Really?'

'Yes. Really. I've had hypnotherapy so I don't get triggered when I see a spider. I can even say the word without breaking out in a sweat. I can look at pictures of them too. I even draw doodles of them.'

'So if you turned and saw that big spider hanging from the picture rail you wouldn't scream and throw yourself into my arms?'

Audrey tried to control the urge to turn around. She used every technique she'd been taught. She could cope with cobwebs. Sure, she could. They were pretty in a weird sort of way. Like lace… or something.

She was *not* going to have a totally embarrassing panic attack.

Not after all that therapy. She was going to smile at Incy-Wincy because that was what sensible people who weren't scared spitless of spiders did, right?

Her heart rate skyrocketed. *Breathe. Breathe. Breathe.* Beads of sweat dripped between her shoulder blades as if she were leaking oil. *Don't panic. Don't panic. Don't panic.* Her breathing stop-started as though a tormenting hand were gripping, then releasing her throat. *Grip. Release. Grip. Release. Grip. Release.*

What if the spider moved? What if this very second it was climbing down from the picture rail and was about to land on her head? Or scuttle down the back of her dress? Audrey shivered and took a step closer to Lucien, figuring it was a step further away from the spider even if it brought her closer to her arch-enemy Number One. 'Y-you're joking, right?'

'Why don't you turn around and see?'

Audrey didn't want to turn around. Didn't want to see the spider. She was quite happy looking at Lucien instead. Maybe her therapist should include 'Looking at Lucien' in her treatment plan. Diversionary therapy…or something.

This close she could smell his aftershave—a lemony and lime combo with an understory of something fresh and woodsy. It flirted with her senses, drugging them into a stupor like a bee exposed to exotic pollen. She could see the way his stubble was dotted around his mouth in little dark pinpricks. Her fingers itched to glide across the sexy rasp of his male flesh. She drew in a calming breath.

You've got this. You've spent a veritable fortune to get this.

She slowly turned around, and saw a spider dangling inches from her face.

A big one.

A ginormous one.

A genetically engineered one.

A throwback from the dinosaur age.

She gave a high-pitched yelp and turned into the rock-hard wall of Lucien's chest, wrapping her arms around his waist and burying her face in the cashmere of his sweater. She danced up and down on her toes to shake off the sensation of sticky spider feet climbing up her legs. 'Get rid of it!'

Lucien's hands settled on her upper arms, his fingers almost overlapping. 'It won't hurt you. It's probably more frightened of you.'

She huddled closer, squeezing her eyes shut, shuddering all over. 'I don't care if it's frightened of me. Tell it to get some therapy.'

She felt the rumble of his laughter against her cheek and glanced up to see a smile stretching his mouth. 'Oh. My. God,' she said as if witnessing a life-changing phenomenon. 'You smiled. You actually smiled.'

His smile became lopsided, making his eyes gleam in a way she had never witnessed before. Then his gaze went to her mouth as if pulled there by a force he had no control over. She could feel the weight of his eyes on her mouth. She was as close to him as she had been to any man. Closer. Closer than she had been to him at the last wedding reception. Her entire body tingled as if tuning in to a new radar signal. Her flesh contracting, all her nerves on high alert. She could feel the gentle pressure from each of his fingers against her arms, warm and sensual.

His fingers tensed for a moment, but then he dragged his gaze away from her mouth and unwrapped her arms from his waist as if she had scorched him. 'I'll take care of the spider. Wait in the kitchen.'

Audrey sucked in her lower lip. 'You're not going to kill it…are you?'

'That was the general idea,' he said. 'What else do you want me to do? Take it home with me and handfeed it flies?'

She stole a glance at the spider and fought back a shudder. 'It's probably got babies. It seems cruel to kill it.'

He shook his head as if he was having a bad

dream. 'Okay. So I humanely remove the spider.' He picked up an old greetings card off the bookshelf and a glass tumbler from the drinks cabinet. He glanced at her. 'You sure you want to watch?'

Audrey rubbed at the creepy-crawly sensation running along her arms. 'It'll be good for me. Exposure therapy.'

'Ri-i-ight.' Lucien shrugged and approached the spider with the glass and the card.

Audrey covered her face with her hands but then peeped through the gaps in her splayed fingers. There was only so much exposure she would deal with at any one time.

Lucien slipped the card beneath the spider and then placed the glass over it. 'Voila. One captured spider. Alive.' He walked to the front door of the cottage and then, dashing through the pelting rain, placed the spider under the shelter of the garden shed a small distance away.

He came back, sidestepping puddles and keeping his head down against the driving rain. Audrey grabbed a towel from the downstairs bathroom and handed it to him. He rubbed it roughly over his hair.

She was insanely jealous of the towel. She had towel envy. Who knew such a thing existed? She wanted to run her fingers through that thick, dark, damp hair. She wanted to run her hands across his scalp and pull his head down so his mouth could cover hers. She wanted to see if his firm mouth would soften against hers or grow hard and insistent with passion.

She wanted. Wanted. Wanted the one thing she wasn't supposed to want.

Lucien scrunched up the towel in one hand and pushed back his hair with the other. 'This storm looks like it's not going to end anytime soon.'

Just like the storm of need in her body.

What was it about Lucien that made her feel so turned on? No other man triggered this crazy out-of-character reaction in her. She didn't fantasise about other men. She didn't stare at them and wonder what it would be like to kiss them. She didn't ache to feel their hands on her body.

But Lucien Fox had always made her feel this way. It was the bane of her life that *he* was the only man she was attracted to. She couldn't walk past him without wanting to touch him. She couldn't be in the same room—the same country—without wanting him.

What was wrong with her?

She didn't even like him as a person. He was too formal and stiff. He rarely smiled. He thought she was silly and irresponsible like her mother. Not that her two tipsy episodes had helped in that regard, but still. She had always hated her mother's weddings ever since she'd gone to the first one as a four-year-old.

By the time Sibella married Lucien's father for the first time, Audrey was eighteen. A couple of glasses of champagne—well, it might have been three or four, but she couldn't remember—had helped her cope reasonably well with the torture of watching her mother marry yet another unsuitable man. Audrey would be the one to pick up the pieces when it all came to a messy and excruciatingly public end.

Why couldn't she get through a simple wedding reception or two or three without lusting over Lucien?

Another boom of thunder sounded so close by it made the whole cottage shudder. Audrey winced. 'Gosh. That was close.'

Lucien looked down at her. 'You're not scared of storms?'

'No. I love them. I particularly love watching them down here, coming across the fields.'

He twitched one of the curtains aside. 'Where did you park your car? I didn't see it when I drove in.'

'Under the biggest oak tree,' Audrey said. 'I didn't want it to be easy to see in case the press followed me.'

'Did you see anyone following you?'

'No, but there were recent tyre tracks on the driveway—I thought they were Mum and Harlan's.'

'The caretaker's, perhaps?'

Audrey lifted her eyebrows. 'Does this place look like it's been taken care of recently?'

'Good point.'

Another flash of lightning split the sky, closely followed by a boom of thunder and then the unmistakable sound of a tree crashing down and limbs and branches splintering on metal.

'Which tree did you say you parked under?' Lucien asked.

Audrey's stomach lurched like a limousine on loose gravel. 'No. No. No. *Noooooo!*'

CHAPTER TWO

LUCIEN HAD TO stop Audrey from dashing outside to check out the state of her car by restraining her with a firm hand on her forearm. 'No. Don't go out there. It's too dangerous. There are still limbs and branches coming down.'

'But I have to see how much damage there is,' she said, wide-eyed.

'Wait until the storm passes. There could be power lines down or anything out there.'

She pulled at her lower lip with her teeth, her expression so woebegone it made something in his chest shift. He suddenly realised he was still holding her by the arm and removed his hand, surreptitiously opening and closing his fingers to stop the tingling sensation.

He usually avoided touching her.

He avoided her—period.

From the moment he'd met her at his father's first wedding to her mother he'd been keen to keep his distance. Audrey had only been eighteen and a young eighteen at that. Her crush on him had been mildly flattering but unwelcome. He'd shut her down with a stern lecture and hoped she would ignore him on the rare occasions their paths crossed.

He'd felt enormous relief when his father had divorced her mother because he hadn't cared for Sibella's influence on his father. But then three years later they'd remarried and his path intersected with Audrey's again. Then twenty-one and not looking much less like the innocent schoolgirl she'd been three years before, she'd made another advance on him at their parents' second wedding. He'd cut her down with a look and hoped she'd finally get the message…even though a small part of him had been tempted to indulge in a little flirtation with her. He had wanted to kiss her. He'd wanted to hold her luscious body against his and let nature do the rest.

Sure he had. He had been damn close to doing it too. Way too close. Dangerously close.

But he'd ruthlessly shut down that part of himself because the last thing he wanted was to get involved with Audrey Merrington. Not just because of who her mother was but because Audrey was the cutesy homespun type who wanted the husband, the house, the hearth, the hound and the happy-ever-after.

He wasn't against marriage but he had in mind a certain type of marriage to a certain type of woman some time in the future. In the distant future. He would never marry for passion the way his father did. He would never marry for any other reason than convenience and companionship. And he would always be in control of his emotions.

Audrey rubbed at her arm as if she too was removing the sensation of his touch. 'I suppose you're going to give me a lecture about the stupidity of parking my car under an old tree. But the storm had barely started when I arrived.'

'It's an easy mistake to make,' Lucien said.

'Not for someone as perfect as you.' She followed up the comment with a scowl.

He was the last person who would describe himself as perfect. If he was so damn perfect then what the hell was he doing glancing at her mouth all the time? But something about Audrey's mouth had always tempted his gaze. It was soft and full and shaped in a perfect Cupid's bow.

He wondered how many men had enjoyed those soft, ripe lips. He wondered how many lovers she'd shared her body with and if that innocent Bambi-eyed thing she had going on was just a front. She wasn't traffic-stoppingly beautiful like her mother but she was pretty in a girl-next-door sort of way. Her figure was curvy rather than slim and she had an old-fashioned air about her that was in stark contrast to her mother's out-there-and-up-for-anything personality.

'Once the storm has passed I'll check the damage to your car,' Lucien said. 'But for now I think we'd better formulate a plan. When was the last time you spoke to your mother?'

'Not for a week or more.' Her tone had a wounded quality—disappointment wrapped around each word as if her relationship with her mother wasn't all that it could be. 'She left the invitation and a note at my flat. I found them when I got home from work yesterday. I got the feeling she was coming here with your dad from her note when she mentioned the daffodils. I'm not sure why she didn't text me instead. I've texted her since but I've heard nothing back and it looks like my messages haven't been read.'

Frustration snapped at his nerves, taut with tension. What if his father had already married Sibella? What if there was a repeat of the last two divorces with the salacious scandal played out in the press for weeks on end? He had to put a stop to it. He *had* to. 'They could be anywhere by now.'

'When did you last speak to your father?'

'About two months ago.'

Audrey's smooth brow wrinkled. 'You don't keep in more regular contact?'

Lucien's top lip curled before he could stop it. 'He's never quite got used to the idea of having a son.'

A look of empathy passed over her features. 'He had you when he was very young, didn't he?'

'Eighteen,' Lucien said. 'I didn't meet him until I was ten years old. My mother thought it was safer to keep me away from him given his hard-partying lifestyle.'

Not as if that had changed much over the years, which was another good reason to keep his father from remarrying Audrey's mother. They encouraged each other's bad habits. His dad would never beat the battle of the booze with Sibella by his side. The battle became a binge with a drinking buddy when Sibella was around. She had no idea of the notion of drinking in moderation. Nothing Sibella Merrington did was in moderation.

'At least you finally met him,' Audrey said, looking away.

'You haven't met yours?'

'No. Even my mum doesn't know who it is.'

Why did that not surprise him? 'Does it bother you?'

She gave a little shrug, still not meeting his gaze. 'Not particularly.'

He could tell it bothered her much more than she let on. He suddenly realised how difficult it must have been for her with only one parent and an incompetent one at that. At least he'd had his mother up until he was seventeen, when she'd died of an aneurysm. How had Audrey navigated all the potholes of childhood and adolescence without a reliable and responsible parent by her side? Sibella was still a relatively young woman, which meant she must have been not much older than Lucien's father when she'd had Audrey.

Why hadn't he asked her how it had been for her before now?

'How old was your mother when she had you?'

'Fifteen.' Her mouth became a little down-turned. 'She hates me telling anyone that. I think she'd prefer it if I told everyone I was her younger sister. She won't allow me to call her Mum when anyone else is around. But I guess you've already noticed that.'

'I have, but then, I don't call my father Dad, either.'

'Because he prefers you not to?'

'Because *I* prefer not to.'

She considered him for a long moment, her chocolate-brown gaze slightly puzzled. 'If you're not close to him then why do you care if he remarries my mother or not?'

Good question. 'He's not much of a father but he's the only one I've got,' Lucien said. 'And I can't bear to see him go through another financially crippling divorce.'

Resentment shone in her gaze. 'Are you implying my mother asked for more than she deserved?'

'I'm now his accountant as well as his son,' Lucien said. 'Another divorce would ruin him.

I've been propping him up financially for years. It won't just be his money he'll be losing—it will be mine.'

Her eyebrows rose as if the notion of his generosity towards his father surprised her. 'Oh… I didn't realise.' She chewed at her lip a couple of times. 'In spite of my mother's success as a soap star, she never seems to have enough money for bills. She blames her manager and he blames her.'

'Do you help her out?'

'No…not often.'

'How often?'

Her left eye twitched and then she suddenly cocked her head like a little bird. 'Listen. The storm's stopped.'

Lucien pulled back the lace curtain and checked the weather. The storm had moved further down the valley and the rain had all but ceased. 'I'll go and check out the damage. Wait here.'

'Stop ordering me about like I'm a child.' Her voice had a sharp edge that reminded him of a

Sunday School teacher he'd had once. 'I'm coming with you. After all, it's my car.'

'Yeah, well, let's hope it's still a car and not a mangled piece of useless metal.'

Audrey looked at the mangled piece of useless metal that used to be her car. There was no way she would be driving anywhere in that anytime soon, if ever. Half the tree had come down on top of it and crushed it like a piece of paper. At least her insurance was up to date…or was it? Her chest seized in panic. Had she paid the bill or left it until she sorted out her mother's more pressing final notice bills?

Lucien whistled through his teeth, his gaze trained on the wreckage. 'Just as well you weren't sitting in there when that limb came down.' He glanced at her. 'Is your insurance up to date?'

Audrey disguised a swallow. 'Yes…'

His gaze narrowed. 'Your left eye is twitching again.'

She blinked. 'No, it's not.'

He came up close and brushed a fingertip below her eye. 'There. You did it again.'

'That's because you're touching me.'

His finger moved down the slope of her cheek to settle beneath her chin, elevating it so her gaze had to meet his. 'There was a time—two times—when you begged me to touch you.'

Audrey's cheeks felt hot enough to dry up all the puddles on the ground. 'I'm not begging you to touch me now.'

His eyes searched between each of hers in a back and forth motion that made her heart pick up its pace. 'Are you not?' His voice was low and deep and caused a shiver to ripple down her spine like a ribbon running away from its spool.

His eyes were so dark a blue she could barely make out the inkblot of his pupils. She could feel his body heat emanating from his fingertip beneath her chin right throughout her body as if he were transferring sexual energy from his body to hers. Pulses of lust contracted deep in her female flesh, making her aware of her body in a way she had never felt before. She moistened her mouth, not because her lips were dry but because they were tingling as if they could already feel the hot press of his mouth.

The need to feel his mouth on hers was so intense it was like an ache spreading to every cell of her body. She could feel a distant throbbing between her legs as if that part of her was waking up from a long slumber, like Sleeping Beauty.

Lucien watched the pathway of her tongue with his midnight-blue gaze and she could sense the battle going on inside him even though he had dropped his hand from her face. The tense jaw, the up and down movement of his Adam's apple, the opening and closing of his hands as if he didn't trust them to reach for her again.

Was he thinking about kissing her? Maybe she hadn't been mistaken at their parents' last wedding. Maybe he'd been tempted then but had stopped himself. It was a shock to know he wanted her. A thrilling shock. Six years ago he hadn't. Three years ago he had but he'd tried to disguise it.

Would he act on it this time?

'Were you thinking about kissing me?' The words were out of her mouth before she could think it was wise or not to say them, her voice husky as if she had been snacking on emery boards.

His gaze became shuttered, his body so still, so composed, as if the slightest movement would sabotage his self-control. 'You're mistaken.'

And you're lying. Audrey relished the feminine power she was feeling. Power she had never experienced in her entire adult life. When had anyone ever wanted to kiss her? Never, that was when.

But Lucien did.

His jaw worked as if he was giving his resolve a firm talking-to and his eyes were almost fixedly trained on hers as if he was worried if they would disobey orders and glance at her mouth again.

'I bet if I put my lips to yours right now you wouldn't be able to help yourself.' *Argh. Why did you say that?* One part of Audrey mentally cringed but another part was secretly impressed. Impressed she had the confidence to stand up to him. To challenge him. To flirt with him.

His eyes became hard as if he was steeling himself from the inside out. 'Try it. I dare you.'

A trickle of something hot and liquid spilled over in her belly. His gravelly delivered dare made the blood rush through her veins and set her heart to pounding as if she had run up a flight of stairs carrying a set of dumb-bells. Two sets. And a weight bench. Before she could stop the impulse, she lifted her hand to his face and outlined his firm mouth with her index finger, the rasp of his stubble catching against her skin like silk on tiny thorns. Even the scratchy sound of it was spine-tinglingly sexy. He held himself as still as a marble statue but she could still sense the war going on in his body as if every drop of his blood was thundering through his veins like rocket fuel. His nostrils flared like a stallion taking in the scent of a potential mate, his eyes still glittering with resolve, but there was something else lurking in the dark blue density of his gaze.

The same something she could feel thrumming deep in her core like an echo: desire.

But Audrey wasn't going to betray herself by kissing him. He had rejected her twice already. She wasn't signing up for a third. And if the gossip surrounding Lucien and Viviana was true, she was not the type of woman to kiss another woman's lover. She didn't want him to think she was so desperate for his attention she couldn't control herself. With or without champagne. She lowered her hand from his face and gave him an on-off smile. 'Lucky for you, I don't respond to dares.'

If he was relieved or disappointed he didn't show it. 'We're wasting valuable time.' He turned and strode back to the cottage and took out his phone. 'Call your mother while I call my father. They might have switched their phones back on.'

Audrey let out a sigh and followed him into the cottage. She'd tried calling her mother's phone fifty-three times already. Even under normal circumstances, her mother would only pick up if *she* wanted to talk to Audrey and even then the conversation would be Sibella-centred and not anything that could be loosely called a mutual exchange. She couldn't remember the time she had last talked to her mother. *Really* talked. Maybe when she was four years old? Her mother wasn't the type to listen to others. Sibella was used to people fawning over her and waiting with bated breath for her to talk to them about her acting career and colourful love life.

Audrey should be so lucky to have a love life…even a black and white one would do.

Lucien left a curt message on his father's answering service—one of many he'd left in the last twenty-four hours—and put away his phone. He had to get back on the road and away from the temptation of Audrey Merrington. Being anywhere near her was like being on a forty-day fast and suddenly coming across a sumptuous feast. He had damn near kissed her down by her wrecked car. Everything that was male in him ached to haul her into his arms and plunder her soft mouth with his. How easy would it have been to crush his mouth to hers? How easy would it have been to draw those sweet and sexy curves of hers even closer?

Too easy.

Scarily easy.

So easy he had to get a grip because he shouldn't be having such X-rated thoughts around Audrey. He shouldn't be looking at her mouth or her curves or any beautiful part of her. He shouldn't be thinking about making love to her just because she threw herself into his arms over that wretched spider. When she had launched herself at him like that, a rush of desire charged through him like high-voltage electricity. Just as it had at their parents' last wedding. Her curves-in-all-the-right-places body had thrown his senses into a tailspin like a hormone-driven teenager. He could still smell her sweet pea and spring lilac perfume on the front of his shirt where she'd pressed herself against him. He could still feel the softness of her breasts and the tempting cradle of her pelvis.

He could still feel the rapacious need marching through his body. Damn it.

He would have to stop wanting her. He would have to send his resolve to boot camp so it could withstand more of her cheeky *'Were you thinking about kissing me?'* comments. He wasn't just thinking about kissing her. He was dreaming of it, fantasising about it, longing for it. But he had a feeling one kiss of her delectable mouth would be like trying to eat only one French fry. Not possible.

But he could hardly leave her here at the cottage without a car. He would have to take her with him. What else could he do? When he'd first seen her at the cottage he'd decided the best plan was for them to drive in two cars so they could tag-team it until they tracked down their respective parents. He hadn't planned a cosy little one-on-one road trip with her. That would be asking for the sort of trouble he could do without.

Audrey came back into the sitting room from the kitchen and put her phone on the coffee table in front of the sofa with a defeated-sounding sigh. 'No answer. Maybe they're on a flight somewhere.'

He dragged a hand down his face so hard he wondered if his eyebrows and eyelashes would slough off. Could this nightmare get any worse? 'This seemed the most obvious place they'd come to. They used to sneak down here together a lot during their first marriage. My father raved about it—how quaint and quiet it was.'

She perched on the arm of the sofa, a small frown settling between her brows, the fingers of her right hand plucking at the fabric of her dress as if it was helping her to mull over something. 'I know, that's why I came here first. But maybe they *wanted* us to come here.'

'You mean, like giving us a false lead or something?'

She gave him an unreadable look and stopped fiddling with her dress and crossed her arms over her middle. 'Or something.'

'What "or something"?' A faint prickle crawled over his scalp. 'You mean, they wanted us both to come here? But why?'

She gave a lip shrug. 'My mother finds it amusing that you and I hate each other so much.'

Lucien frowned. 'I don't hate you.'

She lifted her neat brows like twin question marks. 'Don't you?'

'No.' He hated the way she made him feel. Hated the way his body had a wicked mind of its own when she was around. Hated how he couldn't stop thinking about kissing her and touching her and seeing if her body was as delectable as it looked under the conservative clothes she always seemed to wear.

But he wasn't a man driven by his hormones. That was his father's way of doing things. Lucien had will power and discipline and he was determined to use them. He would not be reduced to base animal desires just because a pretty, curvy woman got under his skin.

And Audrey Merrington was so far under his

skin he could feel his organs shifting inside to make room.

'Good to know, since we're going to be related again,' she said with a deadpan expression.

'Not if I can help it.' Lucien was not going to rest until he'd prevented this third disastrous marriage. His father had almost drunk himself into oblivion the last time. There was no way he was going to stand by and watch that happen again. He was sick of picking up the pieces. Sick of trying to put his father back together again like a puzzle with most of the bits damaged or missing.

He picked up his keys. 'Come on. We'd best get on the road before nightfall. I'll organise someone to collect your car when we get back to London.'

She stood up from the arm of the sofa so quickly her feet thudded against the floor like punctuation marks. 'But I don't want to go with—'

'Will you damn well just do what you're told?' Lucien was having trouble controlling his panic at how much time they were wasting. His father could be halfway through his honeymoon at this rate. Not to mention his bank balance. 'You don't have a car, so therefore you come with me. Understood?'

She pursed her lips for a moment as if deciding whether or not to defy him. But then she stalked over to where she had left her overnight bag and her tote, and, picking them up, threw him a mutinous look that wouldn't have looked out of place on the deck of *The Bounty*. 'You can take me back to my flat in London. I'm not going anywhere else with you.'

'Fine.' He opened the front door of the cottage so she could walk out ahead of him. 'Go and sit in the car while I lock up.'

Audrey went to his car, sat inside and pulled the seat belt into place with a savage click. Why did he have to be so cavemanish about getting her to go with him? She could have had a hire car delivered or got a friend to collect her. Even a taxi would be worth the expense rather than suffering a couple of hours in Lucien's disturbing and far too tempting company. The last thing she wanted to do was to make a fool of herself again. She wasn't eighteen now. She wasn't twenty-one. She was twenty-five and mature enough—she hoped—to put this silly crush to bed once and for all.

Okay, so that wasn't the best choice of words.

She would nix her crush on Lucien. It was just a physical thing. It wasn't a cerebral or emotional thing. It was lust. Good old-fashioned lust and it would burn out sooner or later as long as she didn't feed it. Which meant absolutely no fantasising about his mouth. She wouldn't even look at it. She wouldn't daydream about it coming down on hers and his tongue gliding through the seam of her lips and—

Audrey pinched herself on the arm like someone flicking an elastic band around their wrist to stop themselves from smoking. This was like any other addiction and she had to stop it. She had to stop it *right* now. She would be strong. She would conquer this.

Besides, according to Rosie and her gossip magazine source, Lucien was in a committed relationship. It was weird how edgy it made her feel to think of him in a long-term relationship. Why should she care if he was practically engaged? Was he in love with Viviana Prestonward? Funny, but Audrey couldn't imagine him falling in love. He was nowhere near the playboy his father was between marriages, but neither was he a plaster saint. He dated women for a month or two and then moved on.

She sat in the passenger seat of his top model BMW as he got on with the business of locking up the cottage and putting the key under the left-hand plant pot. It seemed strange that he knew the cottage routine so well. She'd always loved the place because it was something she and her mother had shared before all the crazy celebrity stuff happened. But apparently Sibella had shared it with Harlan and now Lucien.

Audrey waited until he got behind the wheel of his car to ask, 'How many times have you been down here?'

'To the cottage?'

'You knew where to put the spare key. I figured you must have been here before or someone's told you the routine.'

He started the engine and did a neat three-point turn on the driveway. His arm was resting on the back of her seat so close to her neck and shoulders she suppressed a tiny shiver. 'I came down for a weekend once.'

'When?'

'A month or two before their second divorce.' His tone was casual but his hands on the steering wheel tightened. 'They asked me down for the weekend. They asked you too, but you had something else on. A date, your mother said.'

Audrey could remember being invited to spend the weekend with her mother and Harlan but neither of them had mentioned inviting Lucien. She'd declined the invitation, as she hadn't wanted her mother and Harlan to think she sat at home every weekend with nothing better to do than read or watch soppy movies. Which was basically what she did most weekends, but still.

Why had they invited him as well as her? They were well aware of the enmity between her and Lucien. 'Why did you accept the invitation? I can't imagine spending a weekend with them would have been high on your list of priorities.'

He drove along the country lane where leaves and small branches from the trees littered the road and along the roadside after the thrashing of the earlier wind. 'True. But I had nothing better to do that weekend and I wanted to see the cottage for myself. My father had talked about it a few times.'

'So, no hot date with a supermodel that weekend, huh?' Audrey said. 'My heart bleeds.'

He flicked a glance her way. 'How was your date that weekend? Worth the sacrifice of missing out on a weekend with your mother and my father?'

'It was great. Fun. Amazing. The best date ever.' *Stop already.*

'Are you dating the same guy now?'

Audrey laughed. Who said she couldn't act? 'No. I've had dozens since him.'

'So, no one permanent?'

She chanced a glance at him. 'What's with all the questions about my love life?'

He shrugged. 'Just wondering if you've got plans to settle down.'

'Nope. Not me.' She turned back to face the front and crossed one leg over the other and folded her arms. 'I've been to enough of my mother's weddings to last a lifetime. Two lifetimes.' She waited a beat and added with what she hoped sounded like mild interest, 'What about you?'

'What about me?'

Audrey glanced at him again. 'Do you plan to get married one day?'

He continued to look at the road in front, negotiating fallen branches and puddles and potholes. 'Maybe one day.'

'One day soon or one day later?'

Why are you asking that?

'Why the sudden interest in my private life?'

Audrey couldn't explain the strange feeling in her stomach—a dragging sensation, a weight that felt as heavy as a tombstone—at the thought of Lucien getting married one day. 'I could read about it in the gossip pages but I thought I'd ask you directly. Just in case what's in the papers isn't true.'

'What did you read?'

'I didn't read it myself but someone who did told me you're about to get engaged to Viviana Prestonward.'

He made a grunting sound. 'It's not true.'

She turned in her seat to look at him but he suddenly frowned and pushed down hard on the brakes. 'Damn it to hell.'

Audrey turned to look at the road ahead where his gaze was trained. A large tree had fallen across the wooden bridge, bringing down a portion of it and making it impassable. 'Oh, dear. That doesn't look good.'

Lucien thumped the heel of his hand on the steering wheel, then turned to look at her, frowning so heavily his eyebrows were knitted. 'Is there any other way around this stream? Another road? Another bridge?'

Audrey shook her head. 'Nope. One road in. One road out.'

He swore and let out a harsh-sounding breath. 'I don't believe this.'

'Welcome to life in the country.'

He got out of the car and strode over to the broken bridge, standing with his hands on his hips and his feet slightly apart. Audrey came over to stand next to him, conscious of the almost palpable tension in his body.

'Can it be…repaired?' Her voice came out one part hesitant, two parts hopeful. 'I mean, maybe we can call someone from the council to fix it. We could tell them it's an emergency or something.'

He turned away from the bridge with another muttered curse. 'There are far bigger emergencies than a single-lane bridge on a lane in the countryside that only a handful of people use.' He strode towards his car, kicking a fallen branch out of the way with his foot. 'We'll have to stay at the cottage until I can get a helicopter down here to take us out.'

Audrey stopped dead like she had come up against an invisible wall. But in a way she had. The invisible wall of her fear of flying. Flying in helicopters, to be precise. No way was she going in a helicopter. No flipping way. Give her a spider any day. Give her a roomful of them. She would cuddle a colony of spiders but flying in an overgrown egg-beater was not going to happen.

Lucien glanced back at her when he got to his car. 'What's wrong?'

Audrey gave a gulping swallow, her stomach churning so fast she could have made butter. 'I'm not going in a helicopter.'

'Don't worry—I'll clear out the spiders first.'

'Very funny.'

He held the passenger door open for her in a pointed manner. 'Are you coming with me or do you plan to walk back?'

Audrey walked to his car and slipped into the passenger seat, keeping her gaze averted. He closed the door and went around to his side and was soon back behind the wheel and doing one of his masterful three-point turns that, if she were driving, would have taken five or six turns. Possibly more…that was, if she didn't end up with the car in the ditch in the process. She looked at the brooding sky and suppressed a shudder. She had to think of a way back to London that didn't involve propellers.

'I should be able to get a helicopter first thing in the morning,' Lucien said. 'I'd try for one now but I'm not sure the weather is all that favourable.'

Argh! Don't remind me how dangerous it is to fly in one of those things.

'I'm surprised Britain's most successful forensic accountant doesn't have a helicopter or two of his own waiting on stand-by.'

'Yes, well, I'm too much of a bean-counter to throw money away on unnecessary luxuries. I leave that sort of thing to my father.'

CHAPTER THREE

THE SHORT TRIP back to the cottage was mostly silent, mainly because Audrey was trying to control her fear at the thought of having to leave in a helicopter in the morning. Maybe she should have got her therapist to work with her on that issue instead of the arachnophobia. But it wasn't every day she had to face a ride in a helicopter. Surely the road would be cleared in a day or two at the most? It wasn't like she'd be stuck down here for weeks or months on end.

But if the next morning's flight was a worry, there was this evening to get through first. Sharing the cottage with Lucien for one night—for one minute—was not going to help her little fantasy problem. It would be like trying to give up chocolate and spending the night in a chocolate factory.

Big mistake.

When Lucien helped her out of the car, the smell of rain-washed earth was as sweet as the perfume of the flowers in the overgrown garden. She could have got out of the car herself but she kind of liked the way he always got there first. No one had ever opened the door for her before. People always rushed to open her mother's door whenever Audrey had accompanied her to an event but she was always left to fend for herself.

She followed him back to the front door of the cottage, waiting while he got the key from under the pot, doing her best not to feast her eyes on his taut buttocks when he bent down to lift it up. He unlocked the door and swept his arm in front of his body. 'After you.'

Audrey chewed at the inside of her mouth and tried to ignore the prickling shiver moving over her skin. Had that spider had company? As far as she was concerned, there was no such thing as a single spider—they were all married with large families. What if there were dozens inside? Maybe even hundreds? Didn't heavy rain drive them indoors? What if a whole colony of them was setting up camp right now? What if they were crawling up and down the walls and over every surface? What if they were in every cupboard? Every drawer? Every corner? What if they were lurking in the shadows just waiting for her to come in? What if one dropped on her head and tiptoed its sticky legs all over her face? What if—? 'Erm…maybe you should go in first in case the spider has found its way back in.'

If he found her suggestion annoying or silly he didn't show it. 'Wait here.'

Audrey waited until he gave the all clear and stepped over the threshold, but even though it was a few hours away from sundown, the heavy cloud cover outside made the cottage seem gloomy and unwelcoming…sort of like an abandoned house, which was pretty much what it was. 'Gosh, it's getting kind of dark in here. Is the power on again yet?'

Lucien flicked one of the light switches but the light didn't come on. 'It could be hours until it comes back on. A tree has probably brought the line down somewhere.' He moved over to the fireplace where she had started preparing the fire. 'I'll get a fire going. Are there any candles about?'

Audrey went to the kitchen—where, thankfully, there were no spiders—and soon found some scented candles she'd bought her mother. It was kind of typical of her that they hadn't been used. She brought them back to the sitting room and set one on the coffee table in front of the two facing sofas and the other one on the antique sideboard. 'These should do the job.'

'Perfect.' Lucien came over with the box of matches and lit the candles and soon the fragrance of patchouli and honeysuckle wafted through the air.

Audrey couldn't stop staring at his features in the muted glow of the candlelight. His skin was olive-toned and tanned as if he had holidayed in the sun recently. The flickering shadows highlighted the planes and contours of his face: the uncompromising jaw, the strong blade of a nose, the prominent dark eyebrows and those amazing midnight-blue eyes.

But it was his mouth that always lured her gaze like a yo-yo dieter to a cake counter. His mouth was both firm and yet sensual with well-defined vermillion borders that made her wonder what a kiss from him would be like. Would those firm lips soften or harden in passion? Would they crush or cajole? Would they evoke a storm of need in her that so far she had only ever dreamed about experiencing?

'Is something wrong?' Lucien frowned.

Audrey did a rapid blink and rocked back on her heels…well, not heels exactly. She was wearing ballet flats. Although, given that Lucien was so tall, maybe she should have worn stilettos… or maybe a pair of stilts. 'Have you been on holiday recently?'

'I spent Easter in Barbados.'

She gave a little laugh with a grace note of envy. 'Of course.'

His frown deepened. 'Why "of course"?'

Audrey gave an off-hand shrug and bent down

to tidy the out-of-date magazines on the coffee table. 'Did you go with Viviana Prestonward?'

'I went to see a client there. Not that it's any of your or anyone's business.'

She straightened from the coffee table and turned back to look at him. 'Just asking. There's no need to be so antsy about it.'

He turned to face the fire, stirring it so savagely with the poker the flames leapt and danced. 'I'm not a rock star like my father. I don't like my private life being splashed over every paper or online forum.' He put the poker back in its stand and turned around to look at her. 'Does it happen to you? The press interest?'

Audrey sat on the edge of the sofa and played with the fringe of the rug with her foot. 'Not much, but then, I'm way too boring. Who wants to know what a library archivist gets up to in her spare time?'

His gaze became thoughtful. 'What do you get up to?'

Audrey sat back on the sofa, and, picking up one of the scatter cushions, cuddled it against her stomach. 'I read, I watch TV, go to the occasional movie.' She made a rueful twist of her mouth. 'See? Boring.'

'What about boyfriends? Those dozens of lovers you were telling me about earlier.'

Audrey knew if she kept going with this conversation her hot cheeks would be giving the fire in the grate some serious competition. She tossed the cushion to one side and rose from the sofa in one movement that was supposed to be agile and graceful as a supermodel's, but her foot snagged on the rug and she banged her shin on the coffee table. 'Ouch!' She clapped a hand to her leg and did a hopping dance as the pain pulsated through her shinbone. The scented candle flickered from the impact but thankfully remained upright.

Lucien came across and steadied her with his hands on her upper arms. 'Are you okay? Did it break the skin?'

'I'm fine. It's just a bump.'

He bent down in front of her and inspected her shin; his warm, dry hand so gentle on her leg she couldn't decide if it felt like a tickle or a caress—maybe it was a bit of both. The sensation of his fingers on her bare flesh stirred her senses, making her aware of each broad pad of his fingers. She suddenly became aware of the intimacy of his position in front of her. His face was level with her pelvis and her mind raced with a host of erotic images of him kissing her, touching her…*there.*

'You're going to bruise—you're starting to already.' His fingertip traced over the red mark on her shin as softly as a feather on a priceless object.

Audrey held her breath for so long she thought she might faint. Or maybe it was because no man had ever knelt down in front of her and touched her with such gentleness. Or maybe it was because she had never felt so aware of her body before—how each cell seemed to swell and throb with a need for more of his touch. Now that he'd touched her it awakened a feverish desire in her for more. What if he was to run his hands further up her legs…up her thighs?

To the very heart of her femininity? What if he was to peel down her knickers and—?

Stop it right there.

There was no way she was going to act on her crush. No more clumsy attempts at flirting. No more making a gauche fool of herself. She would be sensible and mature about this. 'You can get up now.' She injected a hint of wryness into her voice. 'Unless you want to rehearse your proposal to Viviana while you're down there?'

Lucien rose from his kneeling position, his mouth so flat and hard it looked like paper-thin sheets of steel. 'I'm not proposing to anyone. You need to put some ice on that bruise. I'll get some from the kitchen.'

Lucien opened the small freezer compartment of the fridge in the kitchen and considered squeezing himself in there to cool off. Okay, so it was a little crazy to go down on bended knee in front of Audrey. Even crazier to touch her but she'd hurt herself and he'd felt compelled to do the Boy Scout thing. It was what any decent man would do…although nothing about his reaction to touching her was decent. As soon as he touched her he felt it. The little zing of electricity that he'd never felt with anyone else.

There was a simple solution: he had to stop touching her. He would keep his distance.

How hard could it be?

He took some ice cubes out of the tray and wrapped them in a tea towel and went back to the sitting room. 'Here we go.' He handed her the ice pack, taking care not to touch her fingers. See? Easy. No touching.

Audrey pressed the pack to her shin, her small white teeth nibbling at her lower lip like a mouse at wainscoting. After a moment she glanced up at him but her eyes didn't quite connect with his gaze. 'So…what do you love about her?'

Lucien looked at her blankly. 'Pardon?'

This time her gaze was direct. 'Viviana. The woman you've been dating longer than anyone else. What do you love about her?'

He knew whatever answer he gave was going to be the wrong one because he wasn't in a relationship per se with Viviana. He had got to know her after doing some accounting work for her father and they'd struck up a casual friendship. It was a charade he was helping her maintain after being cheated on and then dumped by her boyfriend. He had seen far too many relationships—most of them his father's—start in love and end in hate. If and when it came time for him to settle down, he was going for the middle ground: mutual respect, common interests, compatibility. 'I don't have that type of relationship with her.'

Audrey's eyes widened so far it looked like her eyelids were doing Pilates. 'What? But you've been dating her for weeks and weeks. Everyone assumes she's The One.'

Lucien moved across to the fire and put on another log of wood. He considered telling her he had no such plans to marry Viviana but he realised the protection of a 'relationship' could serve him well when dealing with Audrey. Or at least he hoped it would. 'For the record, I don't consider romantic love to be the most important factor in a marriage. That sort of love never lasts. You only have to look at your mother and my father to see that.'

She put the ice pack on the coffee table, a frown troubling her brow. 'Is she in love with you?'

'We get on well and—'

'You get on well?' Audrey let out a laugh that had a jarring chord of scorn. 'So that's all it takes to have a successful marriage? Silly me for thinking for all these years the couple had to actually fall in love with one another, care for each other and want the best for each other.'

'You might want to save your lecture for your mother,' Lucien said. 'How many times has she fallen in and out of love now?'

Her creamy skin became tinged with pink high on her cheekbones and her generous mouth tightened. 'We're not talking about my mother. We're talking about you. Why are you going to marry someone you're not in love with? I mean, who *does* that?'

Lucien straightened one of the trinkets on the

mantelpiece. 'Look, we're clearly never going to agree on this, so why don't we change the subject?'

'I'm not finished discussing it,' Audrey said. 'Why would a beautiful-looking woman like Viviana settle for a man who doesn't love her? Oh, I get it.' She tapped the side of her head as if congratulating her brain for coming up with the answer. 'She's only with you because you're the son of a famous rock star, right?'

'Wrong.' He gave her an on-off movement of his lips that could just scrape in as a smile. 'She didn't know who my father was when we first met.' Which was a certain part—the main part—of Viviana's appeal to him as a friend. He was tired of the groupies and sycophants who only wanted to hang around him because of who his father was. He'd been weeding them out since he was a teenager, trying to decide who was genuinely interested in him or just along for the vicarious brush with celebrity.

Audrey got off the sofa and limped across to the window to check on the weather. 'Well, either way, I think you're both making a big mistake. People who get married should love each other at the very least.'

'But you're never getting married, correct?' Lucien decided it was time to direct the questions back at her to take the heat off him.

Her gaze moved to the left of his. 'No.'

'But what if you fall in love?'

Her teeth did that little lip-chewing thing again that never failed to draw his gaze. 'I can't see that happening anytime soon.'

'But what if a guy falls in love with you and wants to marry you?'

She gave a laugh that wasn't quite a laugh. 'And how will I know it's me they're in love with or whether they want to meet my mother?'

Lucien frowned. 'Has that actually happened?'

She made a wry sideways movement of her mouth. 'Enough times to be annoying.' She moved back to the sofa and plumped up one of the scatter cushions she'd been hugging earlier. 'But then, I'm hardly in the same league as my mother in the looks department.'

Lucien wondered if her low self-esteem came from having such a glamorous mother. Sibella was absolutely stunning; even he had to admit that. It was no wonder his father kept going back to her like a drug he couldn't resist. Had it been difficult for Audrey growing up in her mother's shadow? Had she been compared to her mother and found lacking? He knew the press could be merciless in how they portrayed celebrities, but even family members often came in for a serve at times. He tried to recall any articles that involved Audrey but, since he generally shied away from reading the gossip pages, he drew a blank. 'You have no need to run yourself down.'

'At least you look like your father.'

Lucien thought about the lifestyle that had wreaked so much havoc on his father's once good-looking features. 'I'm not sure if that's meant to be a compliment or not. And, just for the record, your mother's looks don't do it for me, okay?'

Audrey's smile looked a little forced. 'Good to know.'

There was a strange little silence. Strange because Lucien couldn't stop looking at her girl-next-door features with those big brown eyes and her generous mouth and thinking about how naturally pretty she was. Understated and unadorned but still captivating. She reminded him of a painting he had glanced at once without really seeing, only to revisit it on another occasion and being stunned by its subtle beauty and hidden depths.

She had barely any make-up on and her skin had a healthy peaches and cream glow. Her dark brown hair had chestnut highlights that looked so natural he assumed they probably were. She didn't have the show-stopping beauty of her mother, and in a crowd you would miss her at first glance, but she was one of those women whose looks grew on you the more you looked at her. She had hardly changed since she was eighteen, although her figure had developed a little more. He wouldn't be worthy of his testosterone if he hadn't noticed the way her breasts filled out her clothes.

The sound of a phone ringing broke the silence and Audrey turned and fished for her mobile in her bag on the floor near the sofa. She glanced at the screen and mouthed 'It's my mother' before she answered. 'Mum? Where are you? I've called you a thousand times.'

Lucien couldn't hear the other side of the conversation but he could get the gist of it from Audrey's answers. 'What? How did you know I'm at Bramble Cottage? I… I'm with Lucien.' She turned her back to him and continued in a hushed voice. 'Nothing's going on. How could you think—? Look, will you please just tell me where *you* are?' Her hand was so tight around her phone he could see the whitening of her knuckles. 'I know you want to spend time alone with Harlan but—' She let out an unladylike curse and tossed the phone onto the sofa. She turned around and her shoulders went down on a defeated sigh. 'She wouldn't tell me a thing.'

'Nothing at all?'

She lifted her hands in a helpless gesture. 'She kept dodging the question.' Her forehead creased. 'But I've just had a thought. Remember that chateau they rented during their first marriage for your father's birthday in St Remy in Provence? She told me once it was one of her favourite places. Wasn't it one of his favourites too? What if they've gone there? It's a perfect hideaway. They used to go there quite a lot together.'

Lucien remembered the chateau more than he wanted to. He had attended the party for a short time more out of duty than any desire to celebrate his father's birthday. It was one of those parties where there was a lot of alcohol and loud music and a fair bit of debauchery. He remembered Audrey's mother doing a striptease—her birthday present to his father—and feeling embarrassed for Audrey, who'd left the room with her cheeks flaming. He wished now he'd gone in search of her and offered her some sort of comfort, but he'd been wary of being alone with her since the wedding, where she had made that tipsy pass at him. 'Did your mother give any other clue? What did she actually say?'

'She knew I was at the cottage.'

'How did she know that?'

'Phone app. She's blocked me from finding her but she can find me just by clicking on the app.' Her cheeks became a light shade of pink. 'She thought…well, never mind what she thought.'

'Was she drunk?'

Her eyes flicked away from his, her cheeks darkening. 'No, I don't think so… I got the feeling she and your dad just want to be left on their own for a bit.'

'Unusual since they both love nothing more than an audience.'

'Maybe they've both changed…' Her teeth sank into her lip, her brow still wrinkled as if she was mulling over something deeply puzzling.

Lucien had spent the last twenty-four years of his life hoping his father would change. He'd lost count of the number of times he'd been disappointed by his father's irresponsible and reckless behaviour and things didn't get much more irresponsible and reckless than remarrying Sibella Merrington. Sibella wasn't the person to help his father change. She was the one who kept him from changing. She encouraged every bad habit and, after the last time, Lucien was not going to sign up for another clean-up operation.

After the last divorce, it had taken him months to get his father back on his feet without two daily bottles of vodka on board. Numerous times he had come to his father's house and found him blackout drunk. He'd tried everything to get him into rehab but his father always refused. His doctors had warned his father his drinking had to stop or he would suffer irreparable damage to his already struggling liver. Even if Lucien had to fly to every city and village across Europe he would not stop until he found his father and put a stop to this madness. 'Yeah, well, next time you see a leopard running around without its spots, be sure to let me know.'

CHAPTER FOUR

AUDREY WENT TO the kitchen to see about some food for dinner in the pantry, where basic non-perishable items were stored. She lit another candle for the kitchen table and set to making a meal. Lucien was still in the sitting room, making the arrangements for a helicopter—*gulp*—to pick them up the following morning. She thought back over her brief conversation with her mother. She had teased her about being at the cottage with Lucien, but along with the teasing there had been a veiled warning about how far from his type she was.

As if she needed to be reminded.

Audrey had assembled a plate of crackers and a makeshift pâté of tinned tuna and sweetcorn when Lucien came into the kitchen. 'I'm sorry there isn't a gourmet meal on offer but most of the stuff in the pantry is past its use-by date. This is the best I could do.'

'It's fine. You needn't have bothered.'

'There's wine in the fridge.' Audrey nodded her head in the fridge's direction. 'It's cold even though the power's still off.'

Lucien took out a bottle of white wine and held it aloft. 'Will you join me?'

Audrey would have loved a glass of wine but she was worried she might make a fool of herself again. 'No, thanks. I'll stick to water.' She carried the meal on a platter to the scrubbed pine table and privately marvelled at how cosy it looked in spite of the meagre fare.

Lucien waited until she was seated and then he joined her at the table. He had poured himself a glass of wine but so far hadn't taken a sip. He picked up one of the crackers and took a bite and grimaced.

'Sorry, I know they're a bit stale,' Audrey said. 'I don't think my mother's been here for ages. I don't think anyone's been here, not even the caretaker.' She sighed and picked up a cracker. 'She probably forgot to pay him or something.'

Lucien took a sip of his wine and then put the glass down. 'Why does she keep the place if it's empty most of the time? Wouldn't it be better to sell it?'

Audrey thought about losing the cottage, losing the one place where she had felt close to her mother. Something tightened in her chest like a hand pressing down on her lungs. She knew it made financial sense to sell the cottage. But if it was sold that part of her life with her mother would be lost for ever and there would be no hope of reclaiming it. 'I've always talked her out of it.'

'Why?'

Audrey pushed a crumb on her plate with her fingertip. 'She bought it when she got her first role on television. We used to come down here just about every weekend. I loved the garden after living in a council flat. It was like a secret scented paradise. I'd spend hours making daisy chains with her and flower garlands for our hair. We even used to cook stuff together. She wasn't a great cook but it was a lot of fun…' She smiled at the memory. 'Messy fun…' She stopped speaking and looked up to see him studying her with a thoughtful expression on his face and her smile fell away. 'Sorry for rambling.'

'Don't apologise.' His voice had a gravelly note to it.

Audrey looked back down at the crumb on her plate rather than meet his gaze. 'She wasn't always so…so over the top. Becoming a celebrity changed her.'

'In what way?'

She glanced at him again and saw something she had never seen in his gaze before—compassion. It made the walls and boundaries she had built around herself shiver against their foundations. 'Well…she didn't always drink so much.'

'Do you worry about her drinking?'

'All the time.' Audrey's shoulders drooped. 'I've suggested rehab but she won't go. She doesn't see that she has a problem. So far it hasn't interfered with her work on the show but how soon before it does? I keep worrying someone will smell it on her breath when she turns up for a shoot. Especially now she's back with your father. Sorry. I don't mean to blame him but—'

'It's fine.' His tight smile was more of a grimace. 'They're a bad influence on each other, which is why we have to do whatever we can to put a stop to them marrying again.'

'But what if we can't stop them? What if they get married and then go through yet another hideous break-up and divorce? What then?'

His features clouded as if he was thinking back to the previous two divorces. Then his gaze refocused on hers. 'How did your mother handle the break-ups?'

Audrey sighed. 'Badly.'

He frowned. 'But wasn't she the one to end their relationship both times?'

'I guess it doesn't matter who ends it, a break-up is still a break-up,' Audrey said. 'She drank. A lot. She hid from the press at my flat for three weeks last time. I was worried sick about her, especially when she…' She bit off the rest of her sentence. She hadn't told anyone about her mother's overdoses. Her mother had begged her not to tell anyone in case it got leaked out somehow in the press. Why had she kept her promise?

Because inside her there was still that small child who loved being at the cottage with her mum.

'Especially when she…?' Lucien said.

Audrey pushed her chair back and fetched herself a glass of water. 'Would you like some water?' She held up a glass but was annoyed to see her hand wasn't quite steady.

Lucien's frown was so deep it looked like he was aiming for a world record. 'No water.' He rose from the table and came over to where she was standing in front of the sink. 'Talk to me, Audrey.'

She couldn't hold his gaze and looked at his mouth instead. Big mistake. It was set in its customary firm line but his evening shadow surrounded his lips in rich, dark stubble that looked so sexy she ached to touch it with her fingers. With her mouth. To taste his lips and trail her tongue over their firm contours to see if they would…

He put a fingertip to the base of her chin and brought her gaze up to meet his. 'What were you going to say?'

Audrey's chin was on fire where his finger was resting. She could feel the heat spreading to every part of her body in deep, pulsating waves. His eyes tethered hers in a lock that had an undercurrent of intimacy, which made her legs feel boneless. 'Erm… I think I will have that glass of wine, after all.' She stepped away and went back to the table, poured half a glass of wine and took a cautious sip.

Lucien came back to his chair and sat down. It was a moment or two before he spoke. 'My father drank two bottles of vodka every day after the last divorce. I thought he was going to die of alcohol poisoning for sure. I'd go to his house and find him… Thankfully he doesn't remember how many times I changed his clothes and his bed for him.'

Audrey swallowed. 'Oh, Lucien. I'm so sorry. That must have been awful for you to see your father like that. You must've been so worried about him. Have you asked him about rehab or—?'

He gave her a world-weary look. 'Like your mother, he refuses point-blank to go. He's been warned by his doctors that his liver won't cope unless he stops drinking.'

'No wonder you want to stop my mother from marrying him,' Audrey said, feeling deeply ashamed of her mother's influence on his father.

'I realise Sibella isn't pouring the liquor down his throat but he can't seem to help himself when she's with him,' Lucien said. 'It's like they're both hell-bent on self-destruction.'

'Their love for each other is toxic,' Audrey said. 'That's why I'm never going to fall in love with anyone. It's way too dangerous.'

He studied her for a moment with an inscrutable look. 'Never is a long time.'

Audrey picked up her wine and took another sip. 'So far you've managed not to fall in love. Why do you think I won't be able to do the same?'

His gaze flicked to her mouth and then back to her eyes but in that infinitesimal beat of time a different quality entered the atmosphere. A tightening. A tension. A temptation. 'Maybe you've been dating the wrong men.'

She hadn't been dating *any* men.

She was too scared she would be exploited. Too scared she wouldn't be loved for who she was instead of who she was related to. Too scared to be so intimate with someone because what if they slept with her and then cast her aside like so many of her mother's lovers had done? She didn't want to turn into an emotional wreck who turned to alcohol when her heart got broken. It was better not to get her heart broken in the first place.

Audrey took another sip of wine. Two sips. Two very big sips, which technically speaking weren't sips but gulps. 'Maybe you've been dating the wrong women. Safe women. Women you wouldn't possibly fall in love with in case you end up like your father.'

His top lip came up and his eyes glinted with his trademark cynicism. 'Right back at you, sweetheart.'

Audrey put her glass back down with a little clatter. 'Mock me all you like but I would hate to love someone that intensely. Your father is like a drug my mother can't give up. She gets herself clean but then keeps going back to him for another fix. It's crazy. It will kill her in the end.' She gave herself a mental slap for the vocal slip and added, 'I mean figuratively, not literally.'

Lucien's gaze sharpened. 'Has she ever tried to end her life?'

Audrey tried to screen her features but just recalling the memories of those times she'd found her mother with a half-empty bottle of pills was too painful to block. What if she'd taken them all? What if she hadn't found her in time? What if next time she took the whole bottle? She could feel her face twitching and her mouth trembling. 'Why would you think that?'

He continued to hold her gaze like a counsellor would a nervous patient. 'It's better to talk about it, Audrey.'

She compressed her lips, torn between wanting to offload some of the burden but worried about compromising her relationship with her mother. 'We have to stop them getting back together, okay? That's all I care about right now. We have to stop them before it's too late.'

'I couldn't agree more.'

Once they'd cleared away the lean pickings of their dinner, Audrey took one of the candles with her and went upstairs to make up the beds. She put Lucien in the room furthest from hers just to make sure he didn't think she was going to do a midnight wander into his room. When she got into her own bed and pulled the covers up, she looked at the candlelight flickering on the ceiling and thought of the times in her early childhood when she had lain in this wrought-iron bed with her mother sleeping in the room next door. She had never managed to be that happy since. Nor felt that safe. The happy memories should have been enough to settle her to sleep but somehow they weren't.

Or maybe it was because she was conscious of Lucien in the bedroom down the corridor. Would he sleep naked or in his underwear? Her mind raced with images of him lying between the sheets her hands had touched when she'd made the bed earlier. Was he a stomach sleeper or a back sleeper? Did he move a lot or stay still?

Audrey sat up and gave her pillow a reshape and settled back down. Her chest suddenly seized. Was that a spider on the ceiling? No. It was just the candlelight. She licked her dry lips. She was thirsty. The wine had made her mouth as dry as a sandbox and she would never be able to sleep unless she had a glass of water. Why hadn't she thought to bring one with her?

She threw off the covers and smoothed her satin nightgown down over her thighs. She padded out to the corridor to check if Lucien was about but his bedroom door was closed. She tiptoed downstairs as quietly as she could, wincing when she got to one of the creaky floorboards. She froze, her other foot poised in mid-air until she was sure it was safe to continue.

The kitchen was bathed in moonlight now the storm clouds had blown away. Audrey got herself a glass of water and sipped it while she looked out of the window at the moonlit garden and fields and woods beyond. Lucien was right. The cottage should be sold at some point. Her mother had outgrown it and it was sadly falling into ruin without regular visits and proper upkeep.

Wasn't that a bit like her relationship with her mother?

Audrey knew she was too old to be still hankering after her mother's affection but it had been so long since she'd felt loved by her. Sibella loved fame and her fans and had no time for anything or anyone that reminded her of her life before her celebrity star was born. It was like that person had never existed. The teenage mum with her much adored little girl was no more. In her place was Sibella Merrington, successful soap star of numerous shows that were broadcast all over the world.

And where was that once adored little girl?

No one adored Audrey now.

She couldn't be sure if the friends she had actually liked her or the fact she had a celebrity mother. There was always that seed of doubt sprouting in her mind, which made it hard for her to get close to people. She always kept something of herself back just in case the friend had the wrong motives.

She turned from the window and sighed. See? A few sips of wine earlier that evening and now she was a maudlin mess, getting overly emotional and down on herself.

Audrey took another glass of water, went to the sitting room and curled up on the sofa. If the power was back on she would have put on a soppy movie to really get herself going. And if there had been any naughty food in the house she would have eaten a block of chocolate. A family-sized block.

She rested her head against one of the scatter cushions and watched the still glowing embers of the fire in the fireplace until finally, on a sleepy sigh, she closed her eyes…

Lucien was having trouble sleeping. Nothing unusual in that, since he was often working late or in different time zones, but this time it was because he was aware of Audrey in the room down the corridor. Too aware. Skin-tingling and blood-pumping aware. He wasn't sure if it was his imagination but he could smell her perfume on his sheets. And the thought of her leaving her scent on his sheets stirred up a host of wickedly tempting images he knew he shouldn't be allowing inside his head. He could feel her presence like radar frequency in the air. His skin prickled into goosebumps and his normally well-controlled sex drive stirred and stretched like a beast in too cramped a space.

You're spending the night alone with Audrey Merrington.

Lucien shied away from the thought like a horse refusing a jump. They were in separate rooms. It was fine. Nothing was going to happen. He would make sure of that. If she came tiptoeing into his room with seduction on her mind he would be ready for her.

To *refuse* her, that was.

Not that he didn't find the prospect of a quick roll around these sheets with her tempting. He did. Way too tempting. Her luscious curves were enough to make a ninety-year-old monk rethink his celibacy vows.

But Lucien wasn't going to make a bad situation worse by complicating things with a dalliance with Audrey. Even if her mouth was the most kissable he'd seen in a long time.

Damn it. He had to stop thinking about kissing her.

He sat on the bed and sorted through a few more emails but he kept an ear out for her returning upstairs. He'd heard her go down half an hour ago. Why hadn't she come back up? He tossed his phone on the bed and wrestled with himself for a moment. Should he go down to check on her?

No. Better keep your distance.

He picked up his phone again and tapped away at the screen but he couldn't concentrate. He let out a long breath and reached for his trousers. He pulled them on and zipped them up and then shrugged on his shirt but didn't bother with the buttons.

He found her lying on the sofa in front of the smouldering fire, her body curled up like a comma and her cheek pressed into one of the scatter cushions. One of her hands was tucked near her chin and the other was dangling over the edge of the sofa. She was wearing a navy blue satin nightgown that clung to her curves like cling film. A stab of lust hit him in the groin at the shape of her thighs showing where the nightgown had ridden up. It intrigued him that she wore such sexy nightwear when during the day she covered herself with such conservative clothes. He knew he shouldn't be staring at her like a lust-struck teenager but he couldn't seem to tear his eyes away from her. The neckline of the nightgown was low, revealing a delicious glimpse of cleavage. She gave a murmur and shifted against the cushion, her dangling hand coming up to brush something invisible away from her face. Her smooth forehead creased in a frown and she swiped at her face again as if she could feel something crawling over her skin.

Maybe she could feel his gaze.

Lucien waited until she'd settled again before he carefully lifted the throw off the end of the sofa and gently laid it over her sleeping form. He figured it was safer to leave her sleeping down here than disturbing her. He stepped backwards but forgot the coffee table was in the way and the side of his leg banged against it with a thump.

Audrey's eyes flew open and she sat bolt upright. 'Oh, it's you. How long have you been here?'

'Not long,' Lucien said. 'I came downstairs for

something and found you lying there. I covered you with the throw.'

She gathered it around her shoulders, using it as a wrap. It made her look like a child bundled up in a garment too big for her. Her brown eyes looked glazed with sleep and she had marks on her left cheek where the piping on the cushion had pressed against her skin. 'What time is it?'

'Four-ish, I think.'

She tugged her hair out of the back of the throw and draped it over her left shoulder. 'I hope I didn't disturb you?'

You disturb me all the time. Lucien kept his expression neutral. 'I wasn't asleep. I was working.'

She rose from the sofa still with the throw wrapped around her shoulders. 'I couldn't sleep and came down for a glass of water. I must have fallen asleep in front of the fire.' She glanced at the fireplace with a wistful look on her face. 'I think you're right though about selling this place.' Her gaze drifted back to his. 'It's a waste for it to be unoccupied for months and months on end.'

'Would you take it over?' Lucien said. 'You could use it as a holiday home, couldn't you?'

She shrugged and shifted her gaze. 'I have a pretty busy social life in town and, anyway, I couldn't afford the maintenance.'

Lucien was starting to wonder just how busy her social life was. He'd never heard her mother or his father mention anyone she was dating by name. 'You haven't thought to bring one of your numerous lovers down here for a cosy weekend?'

Her cheeks developed twin circles of pink. 'I think I'll go back up to bed.' She made to walk past him but he stopped her by placing a hand on her arm. Her eyes met his and her brows lifted ever so slightly like those of a haughty spinster in a Regency novel. 'Did you want something, Lucien?'

He let his hand fall away from her arm before he was tempted to tell her what he wanted. What he *shouldn't* be wanting. What he would damn well *stop* himself from wanting.

'No. Goodnight.'

Audrey came downstairs to the kitchen the following morning to find Lucien already packed and ready to go. 'Forget about breakfast,' he said. 'We're leaving.'

Her stomach pitched as if she were already in the helicopter. In a nosedive. 'What? Now?'

'I've managed to get a local farmer to meet us at the bridge. He's going to get us across on his tractor and then we'll pick up a hire car in the village.'

'So we're not going in the helicopter?' Relief swept through her like a rinse cycle through a load of laundry.

'No.'

'Why did you change your mind about it?'

'I don't want to draw too much attention to ourselves. The fewer people who know we've spent the night here together, the better.'

Audrey's relief collided with her anger that

he disliked being seen with her in public so much. Was she so hideous he couldn't bear anyone finding out they'd 'spent the night here together'?

She bet he wouldn't be all cloak and dagger about it if it was Viviana holed up here with him. He'd be hiring the biggest helicopter on offer and parading Viviana on his arm like a trophy. He'd probably announce it on a megaphone: *Hey, look who I spent the night with—Viviana Prestonward, the most beautiful supermodel on the planet.*

It made Audrey want to puke…or to punch something. 'You know, if it pains you that much to be in my company, why then are you insisting on taking me with you? I can find my own way back to London to do my own search and you can do yours.'

'Aren't you forgetting your car is out of action and likely to be for some time?'

'I can hire one.'

A look of grim determination entered his gaze. 'No. We stick to my plan to do this together. It'll add more weight if we show a united front once we find them. I think you might be right about St Remy. My father's been there a few times over the last couple of years, so it's highly likely they've headed there.'

Audrey rubbed her lips together as if she were setting lipstick. Why was he insisting she go with him if he didn't want to draw attention to them? Wasn't taking her with him going to cause all sorts of trouble for him? 'What about Viviana?'

'What about her?'

'What's she going to think of us spending all this time together?'

A flicker of something passed over his face. 'She's not the jealous type.'

Audrey arched a brow. 'Would that be because I'm not slim and beautiful like she is?'

Lucien closed his eyes in a slow God-give-me-strength blink. 'Get your bag. The farmer will be waiting for us by now.'

Lucien drove with Audrey a short time later to the bridge, where the local farmer was waiting on the other side with his tractor. There was a hire car parked on the other side as well, presumably left by the company for them to collect. Audrey had to admire Lucien's organisational skills, but then she realised how determined he was to put a stop to his father's marriage to her mother. He wouldn't let even a broken bridge get in his way.

The farmer gave them a wave and they pulled up on the side of the lane and proceeded to cross the river a metre or so away from where the bridge had come down. The tractor climbed up the other bank with a rumbling roar and came to a stop next to where Audrey and Lucien were standing. She recognised the farmer from previous visits to the village and expressed her thanks for his helping them.

'No problem, Audrey lass,' Jim Gordon said. 'Hold on tight when you get on, now. The water's not deep but the bottom is a little uneven in places.'

Lucien handed Jim Audrey's overnight bag and her tote and then came to stand behind her to help her get on the tractor by putting his hands on her hips. His touch—even through her clothes—made her senses do cartwheels. She put her foot on the metal step and gave a spring that would have got her nowhere if it hadn't been for the gentle nudge of his hands. She wriggled to take her place on the back of the tractor and Lucien jumped up next to her and wrapped a firm arm around her waist to keep her secure. 'Okay?'

Audrey was so breathless from his closeness she could barely get her voice to do much more than squeak. 'Okay.'

Jim set the tractor on its way and soon they were across to the other side of the river. Lucien jumped down and, once he had her bags off and on the ground next to him, he held out his hands for her. She placed her hands on his shoulders and he put his hands on her waist and lifted her down as if she weighed less than a child.

For a moment they stood with his hands on her waist and hers on his shoulders. Audrey's gaze met his and it was as if someone had pressed 'pause' on time. Even the birds in the nearby shrubs seemed to have stopped twittering. The blue of his eyes was mesmerising, the touch of his hands making her aware of how close to him she was standing. His thighs were almost brushing hers. She could feel his body warmth like the glow of a radiator. His gaze lowered to her mouth for a brief moment, his hands tightening on her waist as if he was about to bring her even closer. Her heart gave an extra beat as if she'd had one too many energy drinks. She looked at his mouth and something in her belly fluttered like the pages of a book in a playful breeze. She swallowed and moistened her lips but the moment was broken by the sound of the tractor being placed in gear.

Lucien relaxed his hold and stepped back from her and turned to Jim. 'Thanks again, Jim. Really appreciate your help.'

'The hire-car people left the keys in the ignition when they dropped it off,' Jim said, nodding towards the car parked to one side. 'And I'll get the wheels moving on getting young Audrey's car towed to the workshop as you asked.'

Audrey felt like a helpless female surrounded by big, strong, capable men who were taking care of everything for her. She mentally apologised to her emancipated self and lapped it up. She followed Lucien to the hire car and he held the door open for her and helped her in.

Once he was behind the wheel, she said, 'If you drop me at the nearest train station I'll make my way back to—'

'Have you got your passport in your bag?'

'Yes, but—'

He gave her a glance that made something in her belly turn over. 'St Remy, here we come.'

CHAPTER FIVE

LUCIEN KNEW IT was probably a bad idea to take Audrey with him to the south of France but he needed her there to make sure Sibella and his father understood how vehemently they were against their marriage. It was a bad idea to be anywhere near Audrey. He had to help her on and off the tractor, but did he have to stand there staring at her mouth like a punch-drunk teenager anticipating his first kiss?

He had to get his hands off her and get a grip on himself.

But he would be lying if he said it hadn't felt good holding her close like that. Seeing the way her nutmeg-brown eyes widened and the way her tongue swept over her lips as if preparing for the descent of his mouth.

And he'd been pretty damn close to doing it too.

He'd been lost in a moment of mad lust. Feeling her breasts within inches of his chest, imagining what it would feel like to have them pressed against him skin-to-skin. Feeling her thighs so close to his, imagining them wrapped around his as he entered her velvet warmth. He had always dated super-slim women but something about her womanly figure made everything that was male in him sit up and take notice. He was ashamed of his reaction to her, especially as he was supposed to be 'involved' with Viviana.

But that was no excuse to be lusting over Audrey. He wasn't like his father, who got his head turned by sexy women even when he was involved with someone else. He was too strong-willed to let the ripe and sensuous curves of Audrey's body and her supple and generous mouth unravel his self-control like a ball of string.

Way too strong-willed.

He hoped.

Audrey considered refusing to go with Lucien to France but without a car and no spare cash to hire one she knew her search for her mother and Harlan would grind to a halt. The thought of spending the weekend at her flat with nothing better to do than watch her flatmate, Rosie, get ready to go out with her latest boyfriend was not appealing. Well, not as appealing as a weekend in St Remy. It had nothing to do with going with Lucien Fox. Nothing at all. St Remy was the attraction. She hadn't been to the south of France in ages.

But when they arrived at the airport in London, Audrey was shocked to find a small group of paparazzi waiting for them. 'Oh, no…' she said, glancing at Lucien. 'How on earth did they find us?'

His expression was so grim he could have moonlighted as a gravedigger. 'Who knows? But don't say anything. Leave it to me.'

He helped her out of the car as the press gang came bustling over. 'Lucien? Audrey? Can we have a quick word? What do you two think about your respective parents Harlan and Sibella remarrying for the third time?'

'No comment.' Lucien's tone was as curt as a prison guard's.

'Audrey?' The journalist aimed his recording device at her instead. 'So, what's going on between you and Lucien Fox?'

'Nothing's going on,' Audrey said, feeling a blush steal over her cheeks like a measles rash.

'Is it true you spent last night alone together down at your mother's cottage in the Cotswolds?'

Audrey mentally gulped. Had someone seen them? Had Jim Gordon said something to someone? She glanced at Lucien but his expression was as closed as a bank vault. She turned back to the journalist. 'No comment.'

'What does Viviana Prestonward think of your cosy relationship with your step-sibling Audrey Merrington, Lucien?' another journalist asked with a *nudge-nudge, wink-wink, say no more* look.

Audrey was sure she heard Lucien's back molars grind together. 'At the risk of repeating myself—no comment,' he said through lips that were so tight you couldn't have squeezed a slip of paper through. He took Audrey by the arm and led her further inside the terminal to the check-in area. 'I told you not to say anything.'

'I didn't say anything—well, nothing you didn't say, that is.'

'You told them nothing's going on.' His hand on her arm tightened to steer her out of the way of an older man pushing an overloaded baggage trolley.

'That's because nothing is going on.'

'You made it sound like there was.'

Audrey pulled out of his hold and rubbed at her arm. 'I did not. What did you expect me to do? Just stand there and let them make those insinuations without defending myself? Anyway, I don't see what's your problem. No one would ever think you'd be interested in someone like me.'

His frown gave him an intimidating air. 'This is your mother's doing.'

A weight dropped in Audrey's stomach. 'You

think my mother tipped off the press about us? But why would she do that?'

His mouth was set in a cynical line. 'Because she loves nothing more than a bit of pot-stirring. The more press attention on us, the less on her and my father.'

Could it be true? Had her mother done something so mischievous in order to take the spotlight off her relationship with Lucien's father? But why? Sibella knew how much Audrey disliked Lucien.

But the more she thought about it the more likely it seemed. Her mother had blocked Audrey from finding her on the phone app but her mother could still find her. Her mother could have been following her movements ever since Audrey had left her flat yesterday morning. She and Harlan were probably laughing about it over a bottle or two of wine right this very minute.

Lucien's phone rang soon after they had checked in to their flight. He glanced at the screen and grimaced and, mouthing 'Excuse me', stood a little apart from Audrey to answer.

She tried not to listen…well, strictly speaking she didn't really try, but even with the background noise of the terminal it was almost impossible not to get the gist of the conversation from the brooding expression on his face. After the call ended he slipped the phone in his trouser pocket.

'Trouble in paradise?' Audrey gave him an arch look.

He shrugged as if it didn't matter one way or the other. 'Come on. It's nearly time to board.'

Audrey waited until they were seated on the plane before she brought up the topic of Viviana again. 'So, she was the jealous type after all.'

His mouth tightened as though it were being tugged on from inside. 'If you're expecting to see me fall in an emotional heap like my father then you'll be waiting a long time.'

'No. I'm not expecting that.' She clipped on her seat belt and settled back into her seat. 'My theory was right. You would only ever get involved with someone who doesn't threaten your locked-away heart.' She turned and gave him a sugar-sweet smile. 'I'm assuming you actually have one?'

He gave her the side-eye. 'I hope you're not one of those annoying passengers who make banal conversation the whole flight?'

'Nope,' Audrey said. 'I like to read or watch movies.'

'Glad to hear it.' He leaned his head back against the headrest and closed his eyes.

Audrey picked up the in-flight magazine but her gaze kept drifting to his silent form beside her. His arm was resting on the armrest, his long legs stretched out and crossed over at the ankles. They were travelling Business Class; apparently he was too much of an accountant to travel First Class. But secretly that impressed her about him. Her mother always insisted on travelling First Class, even when she couldn't always afford it. It was all about her mother's image, how the public perceived her. It seemed such a shallow existence to Audrey and she wondered what was going to happen to her mother when her celebrity star dimmed, as it inevitably would. She sighed and reached for the remote control and clicked on the movie menu. Her mother's star would dim even more quickly if Audrey didn't talk her out of remarrying Harlan Fox.

And, God forbid, it might even be snuffed out completely.

Lucien opened his eyes some time later to find Audrey sniffing in the seat beside him, her knees drawn up, her feet bare. Chocolate wrappers littered the floor and her seat, including one on his seat. She was dabbing at her streaming eyes with a bunched-up tissue—or was it a napkin from the meal tray? The credits were rolling on a movie on the screen in front of her.

'Sad movie?' he said, handing her his handkerchief.

She gave him a sheepish look, pulled out her headphones and took the handkerchief. 'I've seen it twenty-three times and I still cry buckets.'

Who watched a movie twenty-three times? 'Must be a good movie.' He leaned closer to glance at the credits and caught a whiff of her perfume as well as a stronger one of chocolate. *'Notting Hill.'*

'Have you seen it?'

'Once, years ago.'

Audrey gave a heartfelt sigh. 'It's my favourite movie.'

'What do you love about it?'

'Anna Scott, Julia Roberts's character, is one of the most famous actors in the world, but she's just a normal person underneath the fame and that's who Hugh Grant's character—William Thacker—falls in love with, only he nearly loses her because he's put off by her celebrity status. But then he finally comes to his senses when his quirky flatmate calls him a daft prick for turning her down and—' Her mouth twisted. 'Sorry. I'm probably boring you.' She pretended to zip her lips. 'That's it. No more banal conversation from me.'

'You're not boring me.' He was surprised to find it was true. He could have listened to her rave on and on about that movie for the next hour—for the next week. Her face was so animated when she talked, her eyes bright and shiny with her dark lashes all spiky from tears.

'Anyway, you've seen the movie, so…' Her eyes fell away from his and she began fiddling with the fabric of his handkerchief.

'You have chocolate next to your mouth,' Lucien said.

'Where?' She brushed at her mouth with the handkerchief. 'Gone?'

He took the handkerchief and, holding her chin with one hand, gently removed the smear of chocolate.

You're touching her again.

He ignored his conscience and dabbed at the other side of her mouth. There wasn't any chocolate there but he couldn't resist the way her big brown eyes reacted when he touched her—they opened and closed in a slow blink like a kitten enjoying a sensuous stroke. Her pupils widened like spreading pools of ink and she gave a tiny swallow, her tongue darting out to wet her lips.

Something tightly bound up in his chest loosened like the sudden slip of a knot.

He placed his thumb on her lower lip and moved it back and forth against its pillowy softness, his blood stirring, simmering, smouldering. She made a little whimpering sound—it wasn't much more than the catch of her breath, but it ignited his desire like a taper against dry tinder. He brought his head closer, closer, closer, giving her time to pull back, giving himself time to rethink this madness. His madness.

Stop. Stop. Stop.

The warnings sounded like a distant horn—slightly muffled, muted, making it easy to ignore.

He covered her mouth with his and her softness clung to his dry lips like silk on sandpaper. He pressed on her lips once—a touchdown. A test.

But he wanted more. He ached, he throbbed, he craved more.

He pressed down again on her lips and she opened her mouth on a breathless sigh, her hands slid up his chest, grasped the front of his shirt. His tongue found hers and a hot dart of need speared him. He lost his mind. His self-control. Her mouth tasted of chocolate and milk and something that was uniquely her. Her mouth was like exotic nectar. A potent potion he would die without consuming. His lips were fused to hers, his tongue dancing and flirting and mating with hers like two champion dancers who knew each other's movements as well as their own.

He slid his hands under her hair to cradle her head. A fresh wave of lust consumed him like a wall of flame, whooshing through him with incendiary heat. He wanted her with such fierce desire he could feel it thundering through his groin and tingling his spine. He groaned against her mouth, flicked his tongue in and out against hers in erotic play. He lifted to change position but Audrey pulled away with a dazed look on her face. Her mouth was plump and swollen and her chin reddened from where his stubble had grazed her.

It was a new experience for Lucien to be lost for words.

What the hell just happened?

He cleared his throat and made a show of straightening the front of his creased shirt where her hands had fisted. 'Right, well. That must not happen again.' He knew he sounded stiff and formal. Damn it, he *was* stiff. But he had to break the sensual spell she had cast over him.

Audrey touched her top lip with her fingertip, still looking a little shell-shocked. 'You didn't… enjoy it?'

He'd enjoyed it too darn much. 'Sure. But we're not doing it again. Understood?' He put on his stern schoolmaster face, not wanting to show how undone he was. Seriously undone.

She glanced at his mouth and nodded. 'Probably a good idea… I mean, you were really going for it there. I thought you might start ripping my clothes off and—'

Lucien sliced the air with his hand with such force it bumped his tray table. 'Not going to happen.' But he'd wanted to. Oh, how he'd wanted to. *Still* wanted to. 'You and me getting it on is a crazy idea.'

'Because?' Was that a note of self-doubt in her voice?

'Did you just hear what I said? I said we're *not* doing this, Audrey. No more kissing. No more touching. No more anything.'

She gave him a guileless look. 'Why are you making such a big thing about this? I'm not asking you to sleep with me. Anyway, it was just a kiss.'

Was it just a kiss? Or was it the kiss of a lifetime? A kiss from which all past and future kisses would be measured? His lips were still tingling. He could still taste her. His blood was still hammering.

He needed a cold shower.

He needed his head examined.

He needed to straitjacket and shackle his desire.

Lucien's gaze kept tracking to her mouth like a sniffer dog on a drug bust. 'Listen to me, Audrey.' He took a breath and dragged his eyes back to hers. 'We have to be sensible about this…situation. We're on a mission to stop your mother and my father from making a terrible mistake. Their third terrible mistake. It's not going to help matters if we start making our own mistakes.'

Her eyes drifted and focused on a point below his chin. 'I hear you, okay? There's no need to keep banging on about it. I get that you're not into me even though you kissed me like you were.' She gave him a little stab of a glare. 'You shouldn't send mixed signals—it can give people the wrong idea. Not that I got the wrong idea. I'm just saying you should be more careful in future.'

He sucked in a breath and released it in a quick draft. 'Let's just forget that kiss ever happened, okay?'

She sat back with a little thump against her seat and picked up the remote control. 'What kiss?' She pressed on the remote as if she were switching him off.

Lucien settled in his seat and tried to rebalance himself. Forget about the kiss. *Forget. Forget. Forget.* But every time he swallowed he tasted the sweetness of her, the temptation of her. He would never be able to eat chocolate again without thinking of her. Without remembering that kiss.

For six years he had resisted Audrey. He had been sensible and responsible about her tipsy passes.

But now he'd kissed her.

Not just kissed her but all but feasted off her mouth like it was his last meal. His body was still feeling the dragging ache of unrelieved desire. It pulled and pulsed in his groin, running down his thighs and up again as if every nerve was on fire.

But now he didn't have his 'relationship' with Viviana to hide behind, his self-control had collapsed like a house of cards in a stiff breeze. Damn it, there was that word 'stiff' again. He'd needed that relationship to keep his boundaries secure. He wasn't the sort of guy to kiss another woman when he was in a relationship with someone else, even if that relationship was only a charade.

He had standards. Principles. Morals.

But the irony was Viviana hadn't ended the charade out of jealousy because of that mischievous tweet of Audrey's mother's but because she had fallen in love with someone on her photo shoot—a cameraman she'd known for years.

Now Lucien was inconveniently free. Inconveniently, because without the protection of a 'relationship' with someone else he was tempted to indulge in a fling with Audrey.

Seriously, dangerously tempted.

Bad idea. Dumb idea. Wicked idea. It didn't matter how many arguments he put up, his mind kept coming back to it like a tongue to a niggling tooth. They were both adults, weren't they? They were clearly attracted to each other. She didn't want marriage, nor did he.

He had always chosen his partners carefully. No strings. No promises. No commitment. He didn't choose women who made him feel out of control. He wasn't averse to a bit of passion.

He was a man with all the normal desires and needs. But he'd always been selective in how that passion was expressed.

He had no such control when it came to Audrey. He knew it on a cellular level. She had the potential to undo him. To unravel the self-control he worked so hard to maintain.

But maybe if he got it on with her it would purge her from his system. Get the fantasies of her out of his head once and for all.

Audrey clicked off the remote and turned to look at him. 'You know, for someone who just broke up with the person they were thinking about marrying, you certainly moved on indecently quickly.'

She didn't know how indecent his thoughts were right now. Shockingly indecent. But he figured he might as well tell her the truth about Viviana, otherwise Audrey would never stop banging on about his attitude to love and marriage. 'We were only pretending to be dating. I was doing her a favour.'

Her eyebrows came together. 'Friends with benefits, you mean?'

'No benefits. We just hung out so her cheating ex would get annoyed she moved on so quickly.'

'Oh…' Her teeth pulled at her lip. 'That was… nice of you. But weren't you a little bit tempted to sleep with her? I mean, she's gorgeous and—'

'I'm assuming you're currently between relationships or should I be worried some guy is going to take my kneecaps out with a baseball bat?'

Her lips made a funny little movement—a quirky, wry movement. 'I haven't dated anyone for a while.'

'How long a while?'

Her eyes flicked away from his. 'You wouldn't believe me if I told you.'

'Try me.'

She looked at his mouth, then back to his eyes and he felt a strange little jolt. 'Are you thinking about that kiss?'

'No.' It was such a blatant lie he mentally braced himself for a deity's lightning strike.

'Then why do you keep staring at my mouth?'

Lucien forced his gaze back to hers. 'I'm not.'

'Yes, you are. See? You did it just then. Your eyes flicked down and then up again.'

'I was checking out the stubble rash on your chin.' He brushed his finger over the reddened patch. 'Is it sore?'

She gave a delicate shiver as if his touch had sent a current through her flesh. 'You're touching me again.' Her voice was soft and husky, making his body give an answering shiver.

Lucien dropped his hand and curled his fingers into a fist. 'While we're on the subject, why do you keep staring at my mouth?'

'Do I?'

'You do.'

Her eyes darted to his mouth. 'Maybe it's because no one's ever kissed me like that before.'

Right back at you, sweetheart.

'No one?'

'No one.'

Lucien stroked a finger across her lower lip. She closed her eyes and swayed slightly. He moved his finger under her jaw, applying gentle pressure beneath her chin to raise her gaze back to his. 'Stop that thought right now.'

Her expression was as innocent as a child's. 'What thought?'

He gave a soft grunt of laughter. 'You're thinking what I'm thinking, so don't try and deny it.'

The tip of her tongue passed over her lips and she gave the tiniest of swallows. 'How do you know what I'm thinking? You're not a mind reader.'

Desire throbbed through him, a dull pain in his groin. 'You want me.'

'So? It doesn't mean I'm going to act on it. Anyway, you said no more kissing or touching.' She batted her eyelashes. 'But maybe you only said that for *your* benefit.'

'Don't worry. I can control myself.'

One of her brows lifted and her eyes flashed with a challenge. 'So if I leaned forward and pressed my lips against yours, you wouldn't kiss me back?'

Lucien had to call on every ounce of willpower to stop himself from looking at her lush, ripe mouth. 'Want to try it and see?'

Her smile flickered, then disappeared. 'No.'

No? What did she mean, no? He wanted to prove to her—to prove to himself—that he could resist her. It had nothing to do with how disappointed he felt. He wasn't disappointed. Not one bit. Why should he care if she kissed him or not? He was trying *not* to kiss her, wasn't he?

And he would keep on trying. Harder. Much harder.

He summoned up an easy-going smile. 'Coward.'

Even after the two-hour flight to Marseille, Audrey was still reliving every moment of that kiss. They had picked up a hire car and were driving through a small village on the way to the chateau a few kilometres out of St Remy. She kept touching her lips with her fingers when Lucien wasn't looking, wondering how it could be that all this time later her lips would still feel so…so awakened. So sensitive. So alive. Every time she moistened her lips she tasted him. Every time she looked in a mirror she saw the tiny patch of beard rash on her chin and a frisson would go through her. His kiss had been passionate, thrilling, magical. Their mouths had responded to each other like the flames of two fires meeting—exploding in a maelstrom of heat she could feel even now smouldering in her core. She could feel the restless pulse of unsatisfied desire in her body—an ache that twinged with each breath she took.

Audrey looked out of the car window at the quaint village shops and houses, wishing they had time to stop and explore. The tiny village had once been surrounded by a circular wall and many of the charming medieval buildings dated back to the fourteen-hundreds.

Lucien slowed the car to allow a mother and her two children and little fluffy dog cross the narrow street before he continued. 'Did you know

St Remy is the birthplace of Nostradamus, the sixteenth-century author of prophecies?'

'Yes,' Audrey said. 'And the place where Vincent Van Gogh came for treatment for his mental illness. I wish we had time to stop and have a wander around.'

'We're not here to sightsee.'

'I know, but what if Mum and Harlan aren't at the chateau?'

'I've already spoken to the owner. I called before we left London.'

Audrey glanced at him. 'What did he tell you? Did he confirm they were there?'

'No.'

'Then why are we heading there if you don't think—?'

'He was cagey, evasive, which made me suspect he's been sworn to secrecy.'

'But you're Harlan's son, so why wouldn't he tell you? You're family.'

Lucien gave a lip-shrug. 'I don't have that sort of family.'

Neither do I.

Audrey shifted her gaze from his mouth and looked at the view again. She was glad it was Lucien that had started the kiss. It gave her a sense of one-upmanship she badly needed, given their history. His attraction might be reluctant but it was there all the same. She saw it every time he looked at her—the way his gaze kept going to her mouth and the way his eyes darkened and glittered with lust. She felt it in his touch—the way his hands set fire to her skin even through her clothes.

It had surprised her to find out he hadn't been in a real relationship with Viviana. Surprised and secretly delighted. But he'd allowed everyone, including Audrey, to think he was until Viviana had called him, no doubt after seeing her mother's tweet. Did Viviana think he was now involved with Audrey? He hadn't said anything to the contrary on the phone.

But it had always seemed strange to her that Lucien would even want to get married one day in the future if he was trying to avoid love. Even arranged marriages often ended up with the partners falling in love with each other. Or was he so determined his heart would never be touched?

As determined as *she* was?

And Audrey was determined. Steely and determined. No way was she going to fall in love like her mother, losing all sense of dignity and autonomy by becoming hopelessly besotted with a man who would only leave her or disappoint her.

But that didn't mean she didn't want to experience sensuality. To feel a man's touch, to feel a man's rougher skin move against hers. To feel a man's mouth on her lips, on her breasts, his hands on her…

You could have a fling with Lucien.

She allowed the thought some traction…

He was attracted to her. *Tick.* She was attracted to him. *Tick.* They were both currently single. *Tick.*

What harm could it do? They were both consenting adults. He was the *one* person she would consider having a fling with because she knew he wasn't interested in her mother's stardom. She wouldn't have the worry about his motives. His motives would be pure and simple lust.

Just like hers.

Lucien suddenly braked and grabbed her by the arm, and for a startled moment Audrey thought he must have read her mind. 'Look. Is that your mother over there near that market stall?'

Audrey peered in the direction he was pointing. 'Which stall?' It wasn't Wednesday, the main market day, but there were still a lot of stalls full of fruit and vegetables and freshly baked bread and the gorgeous cheeses this region was famous for. Just looking at all that food made her stomach growl. But then she glimpsed a blonde head before it disappeared into the maze of the stalls. 'I'm not sure if that was Mum or not. It looked like her, but—'

'I'll quickly park and we can do a search on

foot,' Lucien said. 'They might not be staying at the chateau. They might be staying here in the village. Small as it is, it's easier to blend into the crowd down here.'

CHAPTER SIX

LUCIEN PARKED IN a shady side-street and then they made their way back to the market stalls. In her attempt to keep up with his quick striding pace, Audrey almost stumbled on the cobblestones and he grabbed her hand to steady her. 'Careful. We can't have you breaking a leg.'

'I'm fine.' Audrey tried to pull her hand out of his but he held it securely. 'But wouldn't we be better to split up and search? We could cover twice the ground that way. We can text each other if we spot them.'

His fingers tightened on her hand for a moment before he released her. 'Good idea. I'll cover this side of the market area and you can do that side. I'll text or call you in ten minutes.'

Audrey started searching through the crowd but her eyes kept being drawn by the glorious food. The smell of fresh bread and croissants was nothing short of torture. She was salivating so badly she was going to cause a flash flood on the cobbled street. She saw several blonde women but none of them was her mother. Right now she didn't care a jot about finding her mother.

What she wanted was one of those chocolate croissants.

She glanced up and down the market, looking for Lucien. He was tall enough for her to see over the top of most people…ah, yes, there he was, right at the other end near a vegetable stall. She took out her purse and, recalling her schoolgirl French, bought one of the croissants. The first bite into the sweet flakiness sent a shiver of delight through her body almost the same as when Lucien had kissed her. Almost. The second bite evoked a blissful groan, but just as she was about to take her third bite she saw her mother coming out of a tiny boutique less than a metre away. Or at least a downplayed version of her mother. She was carrying a shopping bag with a paper-wrapped baguette poking out of the top as well as some fresh fruit and vegetables.

'Mumffh?' Audrey's mouthful of pastry didn't make for the best diction and she quickly swallowed and rushed over. 'Mum?'

At first she wondered if she'd made a mistake. The woman in front of her had her mother's eyes and hair colour but the hair wasn't styled and her eyes weren't made up. Her eyelashes weren't false; they weren't even coated with mascara. Her mother's normally glowing skin looked pale and drawn and there were fine lines around her mouth Audrey had never seen before. Even her mother's clothes were different. Instead of a brightly coloured *look-at-me* designer outfit, her mother was wearing faded jeans and a cotton shirt and a man's grey sweater tied around her waist. And she had trainers on her feet. No sky-high heels.

This was taking stars without make-up to a whole new level.

Sibella glanced around nervously. 'Is Lucien with you?'

'Yes.' Audrey pointed further up the market. 'Over there somewhere. He thought he saw you when we were driving past.'

Sibella grasped Audrey's hand with her free hand and tugged her under the awning of the boutique. 'Tell him you didn't see me. Tell him it was someone else who looked like me. Please?'

Audrey was shocked at the urgent tone of her mother's voice and the desperation in her gaze. 'But why?'

'Harlan and I want to be left alone without being lectured by everyone on how bad we are for each other.'

'But you are bad for each other,' Audrey said. 'You bring out the worst in each other and I can't stand by and watch it all fall apart again.'

A middle-aged woman came out of the boutique and walked past them without even glancing at Audrey's mother. Her mother was famous all over the world. Sibella couldn't walk down a deserted country lane without being recognised. What was even more surprising, her mother seemed relieved no one was looking at her and asking for an autograph or to pose for a selfie.

'Please, Audrey.' Her mother gripped Audrey's hand tighter and her eyes took on such a beseeching look it reminded Audrey of a puppy begging for a forbidden treat. 'Please just give me a few days with Harlan. He's…' Her mother choked back a tiny sob and tears shone in her eyes. 'He's not well.'

Audrey knew her mother was a good actor and could sob and cry on demand, but something about her expression told her this was no act. She was genuinely upset. 'Not well? What's wrong with him?'

Sibella's gaze did another nervous dart around the crowded market before she pulled Audrey into a quiet narrow lane. 'He only told me last night.' Her bottom lip quivered. 'He's got cancer.'

Audrey swallowed. 'What sort of cancer? Is it—?'

'A brain tumour,' Sibella said. 'I'm trying to talk him into having an operation and chemo. He refuses to have any treatment because the doctors have told him there's only a small chance of success and he might end up having a stroke or worse. But I want him to try. To give himself the best chance. To give *us* the best chance.'

Audrey was no medical specialist but even she knew of the low rate of survival for brain cancers. Surgery was fraught with danger even when there was a possibility of removing the tumour. It was a daunting prognosis for anyone to face, and for someone like Harlan, who had never been sick other than from a hangover, she could imagine it was hitting him hard. 'Oh, Mum, that's terrible… Is there anything I can do?'

'Yes.' Her mother's eyes took on a determined gleam. 'Keep Lucien away. Don't tell him you've found us.'

'But—'

'We're not staying at the chateau,' her mother said. 'I wanted to but it wasn't available, and anyway, Harlan decided we had to go somewhere different for a change. Somewhere smaller and more intimate.'

'But don't you think Lucien should know his father's so sick?'

Sibella pursed her lips. 'Harlan is going to tell him himself. But not right now. I know what Lucien is like. He'll try and talk Harlan and me out of remarrying. Harlan wants me back in his life…in what's left of his life.' She gave another choked-off sob. 'We're planning to have a private ceremony. No fanfare this time.'

Audrey thought back to the luxury vellum wedding invitation that had been delivered to her flat. 'Then why did you send that invitation if you're not going to have a big showy wedding?'

'That was before Harlan knew he was sick,' Sibella said. 'He found out last week but didn't want to tell me until we went away together. Please, promise me you won't tell Lucien you've seen me. Tell him I called you and told you we were staying somewhere else.'

'But Mum, you know what a hopeless liar

I am,' Audrey said. 'Where will I say you've gone?'

'I don't care just as long as it's not here.'

'But why did you come here in the first place? Lucien knows it's one of his father's favourite haunts. Surely Harlan knew he would come here to look for you both?'

Sibella sighed and the lines around her mouth deepened. 'It was a risk he was prepared to take because he knows how much I love this village. We both love it.' She swallowed and swiped at her streaming eyes with the back of her hand. 'I guess he thought it might be the last time we will be on holiday together, so where else would he want to go but here, where we've had some of our happiest…' she gave another tight swallow '…times?'

Audrey's phone buzzed with a text and her heart jumped. 'That's probably Lucien, looking for me.' She pulled out her phone and read the message:

Where are you?

'Please, sweetie,' Sibella said. 'Please just give Harlan and me three days.'

There was that number three again. But it was the 'sweetie' that did it. Her mother hadn't called her that since Audrey was a little kid. She didn't like the thought of lying to Lucien but what else could she do? It was Harlan's place to tell Lucien he was sick, not hers. Her mother said Harlan planned to tell Lucien himself. It would be wrong of Audrey to deliver the news he should hear from his father first-hand.

The news of Harlan's illness changed everything. What would it hurt if her mother remarried him? He might not have long to live and at least he would die happy. 'Okay, but I can't say I'm happy about—'

'I'll send you a text now and drop a hint about some other place we might be staying so at least you'll have something concrete to show Lucien.' Sibella put her shopping bag down and quickly texted a message and within a couple of seconds Audrey's phoned pinged.

She clicked on the message. 'Okay. Got it. But

I still feel really uncomfortable about lying to Lucien.'

'Why? You don't even like him.'

The trouble was Audrey liked him way too much. The longer she spent with him the more she liked him. The more she wanted him with a fierce ache that radiated throughout her body. And that kiss… How would she ever be able to forget it? Would she ever stop wanting it to be repeated? She frowned at her mother. 'That reminds me. What were you thinking, making everyone think he and I were having some sort of…thing?'

Her mother had the grace to look a little ashamed. 'I know it was bit naughty of me but Harlan thought Lucien was going to ask that broomstick model to marry him. He'd dated her longer than anyone else, but Harlan knew Lucien wasn't in love with her. Apparently he doesn't believe in falling in love. He must think it's a weakness of his father's that he's fallen in love with me so many times.' She rolled her eyes in a *can-you-believe-it?* manner.

'Why did you send me to the cottage with that false lead?'

'I've had an agent look at it. I want to sell it. I thought it might be the last time you got to go there. I seem to remember you liked it quite a lot.'

Audrey's phone pinged again with another message from Lucien. 'Look, I'd better meet back up with Lucien or he'll suspect something.' She typed a message back that she was at a public restroom. She put her phone away and looked at her mother again. 'Three days, okay?'

Sibella wrapped her arms around Audrey and gave her a big squishy hug, just like she'd used to do when Audrey was a little girl. 'Thank you, sweetie. This means so much to me.' She eased back with tears shining in her eyes. 'We want to keep Harlan's illness out of the press for as long as we can. And I really want to talk him into having the operation and chemo. But in the meantime, I'm cooking him healthy food and keeping him away from alcohol.'

Audrey glanced at the fresh produce poking

out of her mother's shopping bag. Could there be a bottle of wine or cognac hidden in there somewhere? 'Are you—?'

'No,' Sibella said. 'I'm not drinking. I've decided to give it up for a while, at least until Harlan gets better…' Her bottom lip quivered again and she added, 'If he gets better.'

Audrey waited until her mother disappeared out of sight from the other end of the lane before she turned back to re-enter the market area. She saw Lucien almost immediately and her heart came to a juddering halt. The acting gene had escaped her but she hoped she could still give a credible performance.

'Where the hell have you been all this time?' Lucien asked, frowning. 'I was starting to get worried.' His gaze narrowed when he looked down at her mouth. 'Is that chocolate?'

Audrey brushed at her face and her hand came away with a smear of chocolate plus a couple of croissant crumbs. Why hadn't her mother said something? 'Erm… I had a croissant.' She could feel her cheeks blazing hot enough to cook a dozen croissants.

'Was it good?' His expression was unreadable but she got the feeling he was smiling on the inside.

'Heaven.'

'Did you catch sight of your mother?'

Here we go...

Audrey rummaged in her bag for her phone. 'No, but I just got a text. They're not here. They're in Spain.'

His brows snapped together. 'Spain?'

'Yep. See?' She held her phone up so he could read the message:

Having a wonderful time in Barcelona.

Lucien looked back at her. 'My father hates Spain, in particular Barcelona.'

Audrey's stomach lurched. 'He...he does?'

'He had a bad experience with a tour director there early in his career and hasn't been back since. He swore the only way anyone could get him to go back to Barcelona would be in a coffin.'

Audrey smothered a gulp. 'Maybe he's changed his mind. People do.'

Lucien gave a snort. 'Not my father. Not about Spain. No, this is another false lead of your mother's.' He glanced around the market, shielding his eyes with one of his hands. 'I know this is going to sound strange but I can almost sense they're here.'

Audrey's heart was beating so fast she thought she might faint. *Now, there's a thought.* Maybe she could feign a faint. She put a hand to her brow and staged a slight swoon. 'Gosh, it's hot, isn't it? I think I've had too much sun. Do you think we could go back to the car now?'

Lucien took her by the arm and looped it through one of his. 'Are you okay?' He brushed a finger across her cheek. 'You do look a little flushed. There's a café over here. Let's get you something to drink. You're probably dehydrated.'

Audrey sat with him in the café a short time

later, her mind whirling on how she was going to get him out of St Remy without him suspecting something. She'd promised her mother and there was no way she was going to break that promise. Three days. That was all she needed to keep him away. Why hadn't she thought to ask where her mother and Harlan were staying? Maybe they were staying in one of those cute medieval houses. They might even be able to see her and Lucien right this minute. She sipped at her mineral water and covertly watched him as he surveyed the street outside the café.

His gaze suddenly swung back to her. 'How are you feeling?'

'Erm…better, I think.' She drained her drink and smiled. 'Time to go?'

He rose from the table and helped her out of her chair. 'Do you feel up to a little walk around if we stick to the shady side of the street?'

Audrey was torn between wanting to explore the village and needing to keep him out of it. 'Why don't we drive out to the chateau? Isn't that where we're supposed to be heading?' At least she knew her mother and Harlan weren't there and she figured once Lucien accepted that he might then agree to fly back to London.

'They're not staying there.'

Audrey was starting to wonder if he was channelling Nostradamus or something. 'How do you know? I mean, apart from my mother's text, that is.'

'I spoke to one of the stallholders,' he said. 'The chateau is undergoing extensive maintenance and repairs. It's not being rented out at present.'

'Then why was the owner so cagey on the phone the other day?'

Lucien shrugged. 'Who knows? Maybe he thought I was a building inspector.'

Lucien led Audrey outside and made sure she was out of direct sunlight as they walked through the village. It was one of his father's favourite places and he had come here for a month to recuperate after the last divorce. He couldn't imagine his father would ever change his mind about Barcelona. In spite of her mother's text message, he couldn't rid himself of the sense his father was here. He would stick around with Audrey in St Remy for the rest of the weekend.

They wandered in and out of some of the shops so Audrey could keep cool, and Lucien couldn't help noticing how taken she was with everything—the medieval architecture, the flowers hanging in baskets or spilling out of tubs, the street cafés and, of course, the food. For someone who claimed to be feeling unwell it certainly hadn't tainted her appetite. He found it rather cute she was such a foodie, sneaking off to eat a chocolate croissant when he wasn't looking. He couldn't remember the last time he'd dated a woman who wasn't on some sort of diet.

But Audrey clearly loved food, which made him wonder if she was just as passionate about other appetites. He had tasted that fiery passion in her kiss. Felt it thrumming in her lips as they clung to his. Was she thinking about that kiss now? Every time he looked at her, her gaze would dart away and she would bite her lip and her brow would furrow.

Was she finding it as hard as he was *not* to think about that kiss?

'We'd better find a place to stay,' Lucien said once they'd come out of a handcrafts boutique.

Audrey's eyes flew to his as if he'd said he'd booked them a room in purgatory. 'Stay? You mean here? Here in St Remy?'

'Of course here,' Lucien said. 'I want to hang around for the rest of the weekend in case—'

'The rest of the weekend?' Her eyes were as big as Christmas baubles. 'But…but why? I mean, I—I need to get back to London. I can't flit around Provence all weekend now we know Mum and Harlan aren't here.'

'It's all right. I'll book us into separate rooms. Your virtue is safe.'

'Of course it is.' Her voice contained a note of something he couldn't identify. Was it cynicism or hurt or both? 'You'd never lower your standards to sleep with someone like me.'

'We really need to do something about that

self-esteem of yours, don't we?' Lucien stepped closer to brush a flyaway strand of her hair away from her face. 'Do you really think I'm not attracted to you?' It was a dangerous admission on his part but he was unable to stop himself. He did want her. He wanted her badly. He kept trying to remember the reasons he'd put up against sleeping with her, but now none of them seemed strong enough. Maybe they had never been strong enough and all this time he'd been deluding himself he could withstand the temptation.

But now nothing was strong enough to counter the red-hot desire that moved through his body in fizzing currents and eddies. He had fought his desire for her. Fought with it, wrestled with it, battled with it and yet it had been beyond him, because deep down he knew she was the one woman to unravel his control in a way no one else could.

Her tongue came out and left a glistening sheen over her lips. 'You want to sleep with me? Really? But I thought you said—'

He ran his fingertip over her bottom lip. 'Forget what I said. We're both consenting adults.'

What the heck are you doing?

But right then, Lucien wasn't listening to the faintly ringing warning bell of his conscience. He was going on instinct—primal instinct—and reading the signals from her that told him she wanted him just as much as he wanted her.

Her lip quivered against his finger and her hands came to rest on his chest. 'But you said if we got involved it would only encourage our parents.'

'I'm not proposing marriage,' Lucien said. 'Just a short-term fling to explore this chemistry.'

She glanced at his mouth and swallowed. 'You feel it too?'

He picked up her hand and brought it to his mouth, holding her gaze with his. 'All the time.'

Audrey walked with Lucien into the luxury villa he'd booked for the weekend with her body tingling in anticipation. He wanted her. He was of-fering her a short-term fling. They were going to spend the weekend together as lovers.

But her mind kept throwing up flags of panic. They were still in St Remy, when she'd promised her mother she would keep him away from the village. What if he ran into his father and her mother? What if her mother thought she'd betrayed them? It was like trying to choose between two favourite desserts. Impossible.

She would have to have both.

She could have the weekend with Lucien but she would keep him off the streets of the village by indulging in heaps of bed-wrecking sex. Not that she knew much about bed-wrecking sex or anything.

But *he* didn't need to know that.

The more she thought about it, the more it seemed the perfect plan. She would have to give her mother the heads-up to avoid any chance encounters. But, since her mother and Harlan wanted time alone and with his health being so poorly, she couldn't imagine they would be out too much anyway…she hoped.

Lucien led her inside the gorgeous villa and Audrey gasped and turned in a full circle, taking it all in. The décor was simple but elegant and perfectly complemented the medieval origins of the villa. Crystal chandeliers with polished brass fittings and soft furnishings in muted tones of white and dove-grey. Persian rugs softened the tiled floors and the furniture was stylish and sophisticated with typical French flair.

She darted over to the windows to look at the view of the maze of the streets outside and the neighbouring ivy-clad villas. Flowers spilled from hanging baskets on iron hooks that looked as if they had been forged centuries ago. Overflowing tubs of vivid red and scarlet pelargoniums lined the cobblestoned street below.

She turned and smiled at Lucien. 'Isn't it fabulous? I could stay here for a month.'

His smouldering gaze and his half-smile made something in her stomach rise and fall like the swell of an ocean wave. 'Come here.'

Audrey shivered at his commanding tone. Should she tell him she was a virgin? No. He might not make love to her then. He might think her a freak or get all old-fashioned and principled about it. 'Do you mind if I have a shower first? I'm all hot and sticky and—'

'Let's have one together.'

Audrey hadn't let anyone see her body naked since she was twelve. Of course, when they made love he would see her naked but at least she could drape herself with the sheet or something. 'Erm… Do you mind if I have one by myself this time?'

Lucien came over to her and stroked a finger down the slope of her burning cheek. 'Are you sure about this, Audrey? Us sleeping together?'

'Of course I'm sure,' Audrey said, disguising a gulp. 'It's just I have some…some body issues and—'

His fingertip moved from her face to glide in a sensual stroke against her collarbone and then down to the shadow of her cleavage. Her skin was so sensitive to his touch she was convinced she could feel every whorl of his fingerprint. Nerves she hadn't known she possessed shook and shivered and shuddered. 'You don't have to be shy with me.' His voice had a husky edge to it as if he'd been gargling with gravel. He stroked his finger over the swell of her breast and even through her clothes she could feel her nipples tightening. 'You're beautiful. Sexy and beautiful and I want you like crazy.'

'I want you too.' Was that her voice? That whispery, soft, breathless sound?

He lowered his head and covered her mouth with his in a searing kiss that made every cell of her body sigh in bliss. His lips moved with heat and passion against hers—a soft, massaging movement that made her mouth open like a flower. His tongue found hers, tangling with it in an erotic dance that made her skin tighten in anticipation. His hands gathered her closer, pulling her against the swelling heat of his body, making her own body weep with intimate moisture. His mouth continued its mesmerising magic on hers and his hands stroked and squeezed her bottom, holding her tight against his growing erection until she was making whimpering and gasping noises.

He lifted his mouth and began to undo the buttons on her top one by one, his eyes holding hers in a sensually charged lock that made her inner core contract with need. The brush of his fingers on her naked skin as he removed her top made her scalp shiver in a rush of pleasure. He slid her shirt from her body and his hands skated over her breasts still encased in her bra. 'So beautiful,' he said, his thumbs moving over her lace-covered nipples in a back and forth motion that sent a tremor of exquisite longing through her body.

Audrey set to work on his shirt buttons, revealing the tanned, sculptured perfection of his chest—the well-defined pectoral muscles, the flat dark nipples, the light dusting of ink-black hair that felt rough and springy and sexy under her fingertips. She brought her mouth to the strong column of his throat, her tongue licking over the bulge of his Adam's apple, his stubble grazing her tongue like sandpaper. The citrus-based scent of his aftershave tantalised her senses as if she were inhaling a psychedelic drug. The hint of male perspiration on his skin was just as intoxicating, making her long to taste him—every inch of him—as she had fantasised about doing for so long.

Lucien reached behind her and unclipped her bra and it fell to the floor. Audrey fought the urge to cover herself and stood and allowed him to feast his eyes on her. He gently cradled her breasts, touching them respectfully, reverently, worshipfully. She had never felt such powerful sensations in her body. No one had ever touched her that way before and the thrill of it snatched her breath away. He bent his head and swept his tongue over each curve—first the right breast, then the left—taking his time until her nerves shivered and danced in a frenzy. He brought his mouth to each of her nipples, sucking on them softly, taking them between his teeth in a gentle bite that made her legs almost go from under her. He circled each nipple with his tongue as if he was marking out a territory, the sexy glide making the base of her spine shiver like fizzing sherbet was trickling down her backbone.

Audrey was so turned on she could barely stand upright. She tugged at his waistband and popped the silver button on his jeans. The flat plane of his abdomen contracted under her touch and it made her emboldened to go lower. His masculine hair tickled her fingers and he sucked in a harsh-sounding breath, his hands gripping her by the waist. He released his breath in a steady stream as if trying to garner some self-control. He undid the button and zip at the back of her skirt and it, too, fell with a whisper of fabric to the floor, leaving her in nothing but her knickers.

'Do you have any idea how much I want you?' He spoke the words against her lips, dazzling her senses all over again.

Audrey licked the seam of his mouth with her tongue, a part of her shocked at her wanton behaviour but another part relishing in the feminine power she felt to be desired so fiercely by him. The potency of his erection pressed against her belly, so near to where her body ached and pulsed with need. 'I can feel it.' She licked his lower lip this time—a slow stroke that made him groan and crush his mouth to hers.

His hands went to her hips, peeling down her knickers, and he walked her backwards to the nearest wall, pinning her hands either side of her head as he feasted off her mouth. His commanding hold of her called out to something primal in her. When he lifted his mouth for air she bit down on his shoulder playfully, tugging at his flesh and then sweeping her tongue over the bite mark.

Lucien gave a low grunt of approval and eased back to step out of his jeans and source a condom from his wallet. His movements were rushed, almost feverish, echoing the storm of urgency she could feel barrelling through her body.

She wanted him *now*.

He slipped the condom in place and Audrey drank in the sight of him, marvelling that it was her who had made him feel so aroused.

She stroked him with her hand, going on instinct…well, not quite on instinct alone because she'd read plenty of the sealed sections in women's magazines. But reading about it was nothing compared with doing it in the flesh. Even through the fine membrane of the condom, he felt amazing—like velvet-wrapped steel. He quivered under her touch and made another sound deep at the back of his throat and gently pushed her back against the wall.

He ran one of his hands from her breast to her belly and then below. She sucked in a breath when he came to her folds, sensations spiralling through her when he inserted one finger. 'Oh, God…that feels so good…' She gripped him by the shoulders. 'Make love to me. Please do it. Do it now.'

Lucien hitched one of her legs over his hip and entered her with a deep thrust that made her head bump against the wall. 'Ouch.'

He stopped and looked at her in concern. 'Am I rushing you? You were so wet, I thought—'

Audrey tried to relax her pelvis but the thick

presence of him felt strange…as if she was too small for him or something. It wasn't painful now he had stopped but she knew if he moved again it might tug at her tender flesh, which made it even harder for her to relax. 'You didn't rush me at all. It's just you're so…so big…' Could she sound any more clichéd?

Lucien stroked her hair back off her face in a touch so gentle it felt like the brush of a feather, his dark blue gaze intense and penetrating. 'Are you sure you want to do this?'

'Of course I'm sure.' Audrey could feel a blush stealing over her cheeks. 'I'm just a little out of practice, that's all.'

He brushed his thumb over her lower lip. 'I'll take things a little more slowly. And maybe a bed instead of up against the wall would be better.' He began to withdraw and she couldn't disguise her wince in time. He frowned again. 'I'm hurting you?'

Audrey bit down on her lip. 'Not much…'

Something flickered over his face as if he was shuffling through his thoughts and not liking what his brain produced. 'When was the last time you had sex?'

Audrey swallowed. 'Erm…not…not recently.'

'When?' His gaze was so direct she felt like a suspect in front of a very determined detective.

'Does it matter?' She tried for a casual tone but didn't quite pull it off. Yep, that acting gene certainly hadn't come her way.

Something that looked like horror passed through his gaze and his throat moved up and down over a convulsive swallow. 'Oh, my God…' He moved away from her and she had never felt so naked and exposed in her entire life.

Or so terrifyingly vulnerable.

'You're a…a *virgin*?' He said it like it was an affliction from which there was no known cure.

Audrey made a paltry attempt to cover her breasts. 'Not now I'm not. Although… I'm not sure if what we just did counts.'

He opened and closed his mouth a couple of times but no sound came out other than a strangled noise. He sent one of his hands through his hair, then over his face, rubbing at it as if to erase the last few minutes from his memory. He turned and got rid of the condom and put his jeans back on, his movements as jerky as a string puppet. He turned back to face her and blinked at her like someone exposed to too bright a light. 'Sorry…' He searched around for her clothes but ended up picking up his shirt instead and handing it to her.

Audrey slipped her arms into the sleeves and closed it over her front without doing up the buttons because she knew her fingers wouldn't be up to the task. 'Thanks.'

'Audrey…' His voice sounded as if it had been scraped over concrete. 'Why on earth didn't you tell me?'

'Because I knew if I did you wouldn't want to make love to me. You'd get all preachy and stuffy about it.'

And think I'm a freak.

'Did you not think it might be appropriate to tell me I was about to make love to a virgin? I *hurt* you, damn it.'

'No you didn't.' She couldn't hold his piercing look. 'Well, only a little.'

He let out a muttered curse and paced the floor as if he were intent on thinning the pile of the carpet down a few centimetres. He stopped and came back to stand in front of her and touched her gently on her upper arms. 'I'm sorry. I can't tell you how sorry I am.'

'Don't be,' Audrey said. 'I wanted you to make love to me. I wouldn't have let things go that far if I hadn't… I just didn't want you to think there's something wrong with me for being twenty-five years old and still a virgin.'

He stroked his hands up and down her arms in a soothing fashion, his gaze tender. 'Do you want to talk about it?'

She exhaled on a sigh. 'Not sure where to start… I was sixteen when I went on my first date with a guy I had a huge crush on. Halfway through the date he asked to meet my mother. Turns out he was a wannabe actor and thought by dating me he might land himself a leg up to the big time of soapy television. He humiliated me. He talked to all his mates about what a disappointment I was in bed and I hadn't even been to bed with him. We had only kissed the once. And he wasn't such a great kisser anyway.' Nothing like Lucien.

Lucien frowned. 'What a jerk. That must have been so upsetting for you. Did you talk to anyone about it? Your mother? A teacher or a friend?'

Audrey made a wry movement of her lips. 'I felt too embarrassed talking to my mother about it. Men fall at her feet if she so much as looks at them. How could I ever compete with that?'

'Oh, sweetheart.' Lucien gave her arms a gentle squeeze. 'You don't have to compete. You're in a league of your own. You have so much going for you. You're funny and smart and so cute I can barely keep my hands off you.'

'Cute.' Audrey sighed. 'Puppies and kittens and little kids are cute.'

He brought up her chin with his finger and meshed his gaze with hers. 'I'm not talking puppy and kitten and kid cute. I'm talking I want to carry you to the nearest bed and make love to you cute.'

She looked into his eyes and something unfurled in her belly. 'Do you mean that?'

Indecision flitted over his features as if he was weighing up the pros and cons. 'Of course I do. But I'm concerned that you might want something different out of a relationship with me. Something permanent. I wouldn't want you to get the wrong idea.'

'But I don't want anything permanent,' Audrey said. 'The last thing I want is to get married. My mother's multiple marriages has turned me off the whole notion of in sickness and in health and till death….erm…and all that.' She stumbled over the phrase 'death do us part', thinking of her mother looking after Harlan as he faced a possibly terminal illness. She'd always thought her mother's 'love' of Harlan was an obsessional type of love, a selfish sort of obsession that was all about Sibella and not much about Harlan. But after witnessing her mother's distress over the prospect of losing him, not through divorce but through death, Audrey realised her mother's love had matured into something to be admired, to be emulated.

To aspire to and want for herself.

Lucien brushed his thumb over her lower lip, his eyes still searching hers. 'Are you sure?'

She wasn't but she wasn't going to admit it. She stretched up on tiptoe and linked her arms around his neck. 'I don't want a wedding ring from you, Lucien. But I do want you to make love to me.'

His hands cupped her bottom and drew her closer to his hard heat. 'A couple of days ago I had a long list of reasons why I thought making love to you would be a really bad idea.'

'And now?'

His eyes glinted and his mouth came down to just above hers. 'Can't think of a single one of them.' And then his mouth covered hers.

CHAPTER SEVEN

AUDREY SIGHED AS his mouth came down and covered hers in a kiss that communicated not just lust and longing but also something else… something she couldn't quite describe. There was passion in his kiss but also gentleness—a slow exploration of her mouth that made her senses sing like they were in a choral symphony. His hands cradled her face, angling it so he could deepen the kiss with strokes and glides of his tongue that made her insides quake and quiver and quicken with need. She made breathless sounds of approval and her fingers delved into the thickness of his hair, wanting him so badly it was like a firestorm rampaging through her flesh. Her breasts prickled and tingled where they were crushed against his chest, her thighs heavy with desire as they rubbed against his.

Lucien dragged his mouth off hers and began to scoop her up in his arms. Audrey tried to stop him. 'No. Wait. I'm too heavy. You'll do yourself an injury.'

'Don't be silly.' He lifted her effortlessly as if she were a feather bolster instead of an adult woman who had a sweet tooth. A whole set of sweet teeth.

He carried her to the master bedroom of the villa, and, lowering her to the floor, he slid her down the length of his body, sending shockwaves of delight through her.

He brushed back her hair from her face and stood with her in the circle of his arms, his pelvis tight and aroused against hers. 'Still sure about this?'

Audrey stroked his jaw from just below his ear to the base of his chin. 'I don't think I've wanted anything more than this.'

He peeled his shirt away from her shoulders and gently cradled her breasts, his thumbs rolling over her tight nipples like a slow-moving metronome. His touch was achingly light, so light the sensations were like exquisite torture. But then his mouth came down and he laved each nipple with his tongue. She'd had no idea her breasts were that sensitive. No idea they would trigger other sensations deeper in her body as the network of her nerves transmitted pulses of pleasure from one place to another. He continued his assault on her senses by taking her nipple into his mouth and gently sucking on it. The warm moisture of his mouth and the slight graze of his stubble against her flesh made her whimper with wanton need. There was a smouldering fire between her legs and a hollow ache spreading across her thighs and belly.

Lucien laid her down on the bed and stepped back, and for a stomach-dropping moment Audrey wondered if he was going to call a stop to their lovemaking. 'What's wrong?' she said, instinctively drawing her knees up and covering her breasts.

He leaned down and placed his hands either

side of her head and pressed a hot kiss to her mouth. 'Wait for me. I need to get another condom.'

Relief coursed through her. 'Oh… I thought you might have changed your mind.'

He gently stroked her cheek with the tip of his finger. 'If I was a better man then maybe I would.'

'You are a good man, Lucien.' Audrey's voice came out husky. 'I wouldn't allow you to make love to me if you weren't.'

He gave her one more kiss and left the room to get the condom. She couldn't keep her eyes off his aroused male form as he came back in and her body gave a tremor of anticipation. He joined her on the bed and sent his hand down the side of her body in a slow stroke that made every nerve pirouette. He kissed his way down from her breasts to her stomach, dipping his tongue into the shallow cave of her belly button before going lower.

Audrey tensed and clutched his arms. 'I'm not sure I—'

'Relax, sweetheart,' he said. 'This is the best way for me to give you pleasure without hurting you.'

'But don't you want to—?'

He placed a hand just above her pubic bone. 'I want to pleasure you and I want you to be comfortable. That's my priority right now.' He paused for a moment and added, 'As long as you're okay with me touching you like this?'

Audrey couldn't imagine ever wanting anyone else to touch her so intimately. Her body was feverishly excited about his touch, so excited she could feel the intense moisture gathering. 'I'm okay with it.'

'I'll make it good for you but you have to tell me if anything I do isn't working for you,' he said. 'Promise?'

'Promise.'

He stroked his fingers down over the seam of her body, his touch so gentle it was almost a tickle. He parted her folds and stroked her again, his touch feather-light, allowing her time to get used to it. She quivered under the caress, shocked at how wonderful it felt to be touched by someone other than herself. He continued exploring her, moving his fingers at varying speeds, and the pleasure grew—tight pleasure, straining pleasure, pleasure that needed just a little more of a push.

He brought his mouth down to her and stroked her with his tongue, the action so shockingly intimate, so thrillingly pleasurable she drew in a staggered breath and whimpered. He continued caressing her, building the pace and the pressure until she lifted off into a dazzling world where thoughts were blocked out and only physical ecstasy remained. Waves and pulses of pleasure rippled and flowed through her lower body, spiralling out from the tightly budded heart of her. She gasped and cried and clutched at the bedcovers to anchor herself but the orgasm wasn't finished with her. Lucien wasn't finished with her. He kept caressing her, leading her into another release that was stronger and even more powerful than the first.

He waited until she settled with a huge sigh

and he smiled and glided his hand up and down the flank of her thigh. 'I hope that was as good as it sounded?'

'Better.' Audrey touched his face in a state of wonderment. 'I can't believe that just happened. I've never felt anything like that before when I've…' Her cheeks grew hot and she lowered her gaze.

He pushed up her chin with his finger. 'Hey. Why are you embarrassed about touching yourself? It's perfectly natural and sensible because it helps you learn how your body works.'

'I know, but there's still a double standard when it comes to sex,' Audrey said. 'It's still hard for women to own and celebrate their sexual desire. To not feel guilty about wanting to give and receive pleasure.'

Lucien circled her left nipple with a lazy finger. 'Tell me what you want now.'

She cupped his face in her hands. 'I want you to make love to me. I want you inside me.'

A frown flickered across his brow. 'What if I hurt you again?'

'I'm sure it won't hurt now that I'm more relaxed,' Audrey said. 'I want to feel you. I want to give you pleasure as well as receive it.'

He kissed her on the mouth—a deep, lingering kiss that made her desire for him move through her body in a rush of heat. His tongue played with hers, calling it into a dance that was thrillingly erotic. He left her mouth to work his way down her body, pressing tingling kisses to her breasts, her ribcage, her hips and stomach and back again to her mouth.

He applied the condom he'd collected earlier and gently parted her, pausing at her entrance, uncertainty shadowing his eyes. 'Are you sure you're ready for this?'

Audrey grabbed at his shoulders. 'You've made me so ready for you.'

Doubt flickered over his features but then he smiled and lowered his mouth back to hers in a mind-drugging kiss. After a moment, he slowly began to enter her, pausing every step of the way until he was sure she was accommodating him without pain. It was uncomfortable at first, not painfully so but just a tightness that eased the more he progressed. Her body wrapped around him and, while it wasn't as intense as him touching her with his fingers, the sensation eased that hollow, achy feeling. And then when he slowly began to move the sensations increased in intensity and she felt a growing urge, a growing restlessness within her flesh for more contact, more direct friction.

She moved underneath him, searching for the point of contact that would get her over the edge, soft, breathless sounds coming from her throat. Just when she thought she could stand it no longer, he brought his hand down between their bodies and stroked her until she broke free into an orgasm that lifted every hair on her scalp and sent her spinning into a vortex of feeling unlike anything she had felt before.

He waited until the last ripples passed through her before he took his own pleasure. She held him as he thrust and thrust and then he tensed and spilled in a series of pumps that made her own skin lift in a pepper of goosebumps as waves of vicarious pleasure pulsed through her body.

Audrey lay in a blissful stupor, the sensations slowly petering out inside her like the quietening of ocean waves after a storm had blown past. Never had she thought her body capable of such mind-blowing pleasure. It felt reborn, awakened, stimulated into life and she knew nothing would ever be or feel the same.

Lucien raised himself up on one elbow and played with a tendril of her hair. 'No regrets?'

'Not one.' Audrey outlined his mouth with her fingertip. 'It was amazing. You were amazing and so gentle.'

'You're the one who was amazing.' He brushed her lips with his. 'And if you weren't so new to this, I'd suggest a replay but I don't want to make you sore.'

She was touched by his concern for her but another part of her was disappointed she couldn't experience another round of his earth-shattering lovemaking right now when her body was already stirring for more of his touch. He gave her one last kiss and rolled away to sit on the edge of the bed to dispose of the condom. She stroked a hand down his back and then traced around each of his vertebrae in slow-moving circles. 'Do you think that's why my mother and your father keep going back to each other? Because of sex?'

He turned his head to look at her and gave a shrug. 'Maybe. But a marriage needs to be based on more than good sex to last the distance.' He got off the bed and held out a hand to her with a glinting look. 'Didn't you mention something about a shower earlier?'

Audrey took his hand and he helped her to her feet and she gave him a coy smile. 'I had no idea you were so into water conservation.'

He smiled and drew her closer. 'Right now I'm into you.'

Even as Lucien led Audrey into the shower his conscience kept pinging at him. He'd thought they were indulging in a bit of itch-relieving sex, only to find out she was a virgin. To say he was shocked was an understatement, especially finding out the way he had. He wanted to be angry with her for not telling him but deep down he understood why she hadn't. He wouldn't have made love to her if she'd told him up front. He had never slept with a virgin before. One or two of his lovers had only had sex a couple of times before but no one had ever shared their first time with him. He wasn't sure how it made him feel. How was it supposed to make him feel? Wasn't it a little outdated to hold a woman's virginity up as some sort of male prize to claim? But something about the experience touched him in a way no one had done before. Her confidence that he would take care of her needs made him feel as if she had given him a precious gift.

Not just her virginity but also her trust.

He turned on the water and waited until it was the right temperature before leading her under the spray. He was already hard from being so close to her luscious body. How had he refrained from making love to her before now? Her shyness about her body made him determined to show her how much her curves delighted him. They more than delighted him—they ignited him. Firing up his lust until he was almost mad with it. He always prided himself on his self-control. He wasn't a man driven by his sexual appetite. He dealt with his primal needs in such a way as never to exploit or hurt a partner and if there wasn't a partner available he wasn't averse to relieving himself, or distracting himself with work. But with Audrey standing in the shower with him he could feel the throb and pound of his blood swelling him as he drank in the shape of her breasts and the womanly curve of her hips.

He brought his mouth down to hers and kissed her as the shower sprayed over their faces, adding another level of sensuality. Her hands came up around his neck, her breasts and nipples poking sexily at his chest. He slid his hands down her back to cup her bottom, holding her against the throbbing ache of his flesh. Her hips moved against him in a circular motion that threatened his hold on his self-control. He knew he should be out on the streets of the village searching for his father and Sibella, but here he was in the shower with Audrey and all he wanted was to sink into her tight, wet warmth and experience again the head-spinning rush of release.

But there was her likely tenderness to consider and there was no way he was going to put his needs ahead of hers. This wasn't like any other relationship he'd had, which was faintly disturbing…but in a nice way. This wasn't a simple hook-up or casual short-term relationship. By allowing him to share her first time, Audrey had stepped outside the boundaries he normally set on his relationships.

He was in completely new territory and for the first time in his life, he wasn't sure how to handle it. Audrey wasn't a woman he probably would never see again. Even if his father and her mother went through another marriage and yet another divorce, it still left a connection between Lucien and Audrey—a connection not so easily eradicated.

'Lucien?' Audrey pulled him out of his reverie

by trailing a wet hand down his abdomen and he drew in a breath when her fingers wrapped around his erection. 'I want to pleasure you the way you did—'

'You don't have to feel obliged,' Lucien said. 'I want this to be about you, not me.'

Weird how altruistic he was becoming.

'But I want to.' She slithered down in front of him and took matters into her own hands, so to speak. 'Tell me if I'm doing it wrong.'

Lucien couldn't speak. Couldn't think. All he could do was feel the tentative sweep and glide of her tongue over the head of his erection, and then the way her mouth opened over him and drew on him softly at first, and then with greater suction. Again and again she drew on him, her mouth wet from the shower and her own warm saliva, and his self-control didn't stand a chance. He staggered under the force of his orgasm, the pulses of pleasure taking him to a place he had never been before with a partner. Was it the absence of a condom? Was it the more-than-just-a-hook-up nature of their relationship?

Or was it something else?

Something he didn't want to examine too closely. He didn't do close relationships. He didn't believe true love existed except between the title and credit roll of a Hollywood movie. Sure, some relationships survived the distance but most didn't. The only way he could see himself marrying one day would be to make sure his emotions were not fully engaged.

Audrey came back up to link her arms around his neck, her eyes shining with newfound confidence. 'How did I do for a beginner?'

Lucien wondered how could she not feel confident. He could still sense the aftershocks running down the backs of his legs. He cupped her face in his hands and pressed a kiss to her mouth. 'You were perfect.'

Her smile became crooked. 'No one's ever called me that before…'

He stroked his thumb over her cheek. 'Then maybe it's about time someone did.' And he brought his mouth back down to hers.

* * *

Audrey couldn't remember a time when she'd enjoyed a shower more. Pleasuring Lucien had felt so…so right somehow. She had never thought she would want to do something so intimate with a partner, especially if she was pressured into it. But he hadn't pressured her. He hadn't expressed any sense of entitlement. He had allowed her the choice and she had made it and relished in it.

But now the shower was over and they were dressed and Lucien was talking about going out to dinner. Even though Audrey was hungry she knew their meal out would not be simply about food or even companionship, let alone romance.

It would be about tracking down Harlan and her mother.

That was Lucien's mission, not a romantic dinner for two to celebrate their recent lovemaking.

'Why don't we order Room Service?' Audrey said.

Lucien straightened the cuffs of his shirt. 'What would be the point of that? You know how much my father and your mother love to eat out.' He frowned in concentration. 'What was the name of that restaurant they used to like? They used to go there every night because they enjoyed the food so much.'

There was no way Audrey was going to tell him, even though she remembered it well. Her mother had raved about the food and the service and the chef who had asked for their autographs and numerous photos with her and Harlan. 'I don't know… I'm hopeless at remembering French names.'

He picked up the hotel room key card and slipped it in his pocket. 'Come on. We'll have a wander around and see if we can find it. I'm sure it wasn't far from here.'

Audrey needed to text her mother to make sure she and Harlan weren't out. It wasn't likely, given Harlan was unwell, but what if they had decided to go out? Her mother was a disaster chef not a master chef. 'Erm…can you give me a second? I just want to fix my hair.'

'Your hair looks great.'

'And... I need the bathroom.' She gave him a winning smile. 'I'll be five seconds.'

Audrey dashed into the bathroom and quickly typed a text to her mother. She waited thirty seconds for her to read the text but the message icon showed the text had been delivered but not read. She turned on one of the taps and with the cover of the running water called Sibella, but the message said the phone was either switched off or not in a mobile phone reception area.

Damn. Double damn.

How was she supposed to warn her mother if she didn't turn on her phone?

There was a knock at the bathroom door. 'Are you okay in there?' Lucien said.

Audrey jumped off the closed toilet seat where she'd been sitting and pressed the flush button. She washed her hands because they were clammy with panic at the thought of her and Lucien running into her mother and Harlan. 'I'm coming.'

She opened the door with a bright smile in place. 'Sorry.'

Lucien's gaze searched hers. 'What's wrong?'

'Nothing's wrong.'

He glided a finger down her cheek where she could feel a fire burning. 'Are you sure you're not sore?'

Audrey knew if she said she was there would be no more lovemaking tonight. He was too considerate a man to put his needs ahead of hers. But how else could she stop him from taking her out to dinner? 'No, I'm not sore at all… I'm just not really very hungry.' Just then her stomach gave the biggest growl, which sounded like a gurgling drain.

His gaze narrowed slightly. 'Okay. But if you don't mind, I'll go out for a bit and have a look around for an hour or so. If you feel hungry later then just order something to the room.'

Panic was a giant claw tearing at Audrey's stomach, even worse than the pain of her hunger. She couldn't let him go out without her. She couldn't risk it. 'Erm… I've changed my mind. I am a bit hungry…and the fresh air will be nice.'

He held out his hand and she slipped hers

into it. 'Good. For a moment there you had me worried.'

'Why? Because I turned down a meal?'

He studied her for a long moment, a small frown pulling at his brow. 'Are you being completely honest with me, Audrey?'

Audrey tried to disguise a swallow but it felt as if she were swallowing a feather pillow. 'Honest about what?'

His eyes were like searchlights and every pulsing second they held hers she felt her heart trip and flip. 'You seem a little agitated.'

'No, I'm not.' She answered too quickly for it to be convincing.

He took both of her hands in his, holding them loosely but securely. 'What's troubling you, sweetheart? Is it being seen out in public with me now that we've made love? Is that it? You feel embarrassed?'

It was just the lifeline she needed. 'What are we going to tell people about us? I mean, I know my mother already led the press to believe something is going on between us, but now that something is going on…well, what *is* going on? How will we describe it? A fling sounds a bit… I don't know…a bit tacky…'

Lucien's mouth firmed as if coming to a decision in his mind. 'We'll tell everyone we're dating exclusively.'

Audrey mentally breathed a sigh of relief. She didn't want to be grouped with all the other women Lucien had had flings with in the past. She didn't want to be just another name, just another face, just another body to show up in the press on his arm.

She wanted to be special.

She wanted to be special because he made her feel special. His touch made her feel she was the only woman he wanted to make love to. She couldn't imagine making love with anyone else now she had made love with him. He knew her body better than she knew it herself. He had drawn from it responses she hadn't thought she was capable of experiencing. Her body was in love with him even if her mind refused to go there.

Was it pathetic of her to hope his body was a little bit in love with hers too?

The air was cool outside but not as cold as if the mistral wind St Remy was famous for were blowing. Lucien's arm was around Audrey's waist as they walked out of the hotel and, while one part of her was thrilled at being in his company, the other part was dreading the prospect of running into his father and her mother. She had checked her phone for any texts back from her mother but her text still appeared unread. She tried to relax because she could feel Lucien's contemplative gaze on her from time to time.

There were several restaurants along the street their hotel was on and Audrey knew the one he was thinking of—the one her mother and Harlan frequented—was only a couple of streets away. She stopped in front of a quaint restaurant that had a sandwich board on the footpath with a menu of specials written on it. 'This one looks good.' She pointed to the sign. 'Even with my shocking schoolgirl French I can see it has my favourite dessert.'

'There are more restaurants further along this street. Don't you want to check them out first before we make a decision?'

'But I'm now starving and it will take ages to check out all the other restaurants.'

Lucien shook his head as if dealing with a small child whom he couldn't resist indulging. 'All right. Here it is.'

He led her inside and with perfect French he asked for a table for two. The waiter asked if they would prefer a table near the window or in a more private corner.

'Window,' Lucien said.

'What if I wanted to sit in the private corner?' Audrey said once they were seated with wine and mineral water and two bread rolls fresh from the oven in front of them. Well, one bread roll was left because she had already eaten hers.

His gaze met hers. 'You're not convinced Sibella and my father are in the village, are you?'

Audrey was glad the lighting in the restaurant

was low because it would at least hide the way her cheeks were glowing. 'They could be anywhere by now.'

'Have you heard anything since that last text?'

She had to think for a minute which text he meant. 'No. Nothing.' She waited a beat before adding, 'What makes you so convinced they're here?'

He picked up the single glass of red wine he'd ordered and took a measured sip. He put the glass back down with a sigh. 'My father came here for a month after their last break-up. After I got him back on his feet, that is. I think it was what saved him, actually—a month just pottering about the village being a normal person instead of a rock star. He came back looking refreshed and tanned and the healthiest I'd seen him in ages.'

Audrey pushed a crumb around her side plate with her finger. 'My mother really struggled after that last divorce too.' She stopped pushing the crumb and glanced at him. 'I mean, *really* struggled.'

Concern entered his gaze. 'What do you mean?'

She let out her breath on a long exhalation. Why shouldn't she tell Lucien what she had gone through with her mother? He'd told her about the dramas he'd been through with his father. 'She took a couple of overdoses when she was hiding out at my place. Not enough to require hospitalisation but enough to terrify the heck out of me.'

His expression communicated compassion as well as concern. 'What a shock it must have been for you to find her like that. But why didn't you insist on her going to hospital?'

'I begged her to let me call an ambulance or even to drive her there myself, but she got all hysterical and weepy about her fans finding out so I relented,' Audrey said. 'I managed to get her to agree to let me call her doctor, who checked her out at home. He said she had only taken enough to be a bit sleepy and wobbly on her feet.'

His frown was so heavy it closed the distance

between his eyes. 'That was a big risk to take. What if she had taken more than she'd said?'

'I know it was risky, but her doctor assessed the situation. And then I stayed home from work for the next few days until I was sure she was safe.'

'You said she took a couple of overdoses,' he said. 'When did she take the other one?'

'Actually, she took three in total,' Audrey said. 'One a week for three weeks.'

'And you or the doctor still didn't insist on her going into hospital?'

Audrey didn't care for the note of criticism in his voice. 'Look, I did my best, okay? Her doctor thought she would be worse off in hospital with fans trying to get in to see her. He thought it best for her to have some quiet supervision at home out of the spotlight. I didn't want to break her trust, which I might add I've just done by telling you. She's the only mother I've got—the only parent—and I didn't want to damage our relationship by acting against her wishes. The overdoses were a cry for help so I gave that help and I continued to give it until she didn't need it any more.'

'I'm sorry, I didn't mean to criticise—'

'Did I criticise you for not getting your father into rehab? No. I realise how hard it is with a difficult parent to get them to do what you think is best for them. But have you ever considered that maybe what we think is best for them isn't always best for them?'

He looked at her for a moment with a quizzical look on his face. 'What are you saying?'

Audrey wished she'd kept her mouth shut. 'I don't know… I guess if we can't stop them remarrying then maybe we should just accept it. Who knows? If we stop criticising from the sidelines, this time their relationship might actually work.'

'You can't be serious?'

She forced herself to meet his incredulous gaze. 'Have you ever said anything nice about my mother to your father? Something positive instead of negative?'

Lucien frowned as if mentally sorting through

his compliments folder in his head. 'Not that I can recall.'

'Exactly my point, because I can't think of a positive thing I've said about your father to my mother, either,' Audrey said. 'They're not bad people, Lucien. They just make bad choices. And the more we fight their being together then the more they'll want to prove us wrong.'

His forehead was creased in lines like isobars on a weather map. 'So you're saying we call off the hunt? Just let them get on with it and hope for the best? I can't do it. I'm sorry but I'm not going to let your mother destroy him a third time.'

'But what if she doesn't destroy him?' Audrey said. 'What if she's the best thing for him right now?'

Lucien's expression went from frowning to suspicious. 'What's brought about this change of heart? You can't stand my father any more than I can stand your mother.'

'That's not true,' Audrey said. 'I can think of heaps of positive things to say about your father.'

'Go on.'

She chewed at her lip. 'Well…he's a fabulous musician for one thing.'

'And?'

'And he's good-looking, or at least he was when he was younger.'

'And?'

Audrey sighed. 'Okay, so it's a little hard to think of stuff, but I haven't spent a lot of time with him. And I certainly haven't made an effort to get to know him. I've always felt a little bit intimidated by him, to be perfectly honest.'

'By his fame, you mean?'

'That and because I always feel as if he's comparing me to my mother.' She gave another sigh. 'The first time I met him he asked if I was adopted.'

Lucien reached for her hand across the table. 'I'm sorry he hurt your feelings. He can be a bit of a jerk at times. Most of the time, actually.' His fingers stroked hers. 'I've lost count of the number of times I've felt hurt or let down by him.'

'Why do you keep trying to have a relationship with him if you don't even like him?'

He gave a soft laugh. 'Yeah, well, that's the thing, isn't it? I don't like him much as a person but I love him because he's my father. Doesn't make sense, does it?'

Audrey squeezed his fingers. 'It makes perfect sense. My mother drives me nuts but I still love her and would do anything for her. I guess because before all the fame stuff happened she was a pretty good mum. Much better than her own mum because her mother kicked her out of home when she got pregnant with me.'

'Are they still estranged?'

'Permanently because now my grandmother is dead,' Audrey said. 'She was killed in a car crash before my mother could repair the relationship. I think it's one of the reasons she drinks so much when she goes through a break-up or a disappointment of some kind. It triggers all those feelings of rejection. It's also why she draws unnecessary attention to herself in order to be noticed.' She couldn't believe how much she had told him about her mother. About her feelings about her mother. There were so few people she could talk to. Really talk to. She was always conscious of 'tainting her mother's brand' or afraid she wouldn't be believed. But now it felt as if a weight had come off her shoulders, as if she were shrugging off a heavy overcoat.

Lucien had a thoughtful expression on his face. 'That's sad. I guess I didn't consider the circumstances that had contributed to your mother's personality. I took an instant dislike to her because she seemed to bring out my father's reckless and irresponsible streak. But then, he probably brings out hers.'

Audrey gave a wry smile. 'I heard once that people who fall in love at first sight are actually falling in love with each other's emotional wounds. Their relationship doesn't usually last unless they address and heal those wounds.'

He gave a *that-makes-sense* lip-shrug. 'Interesting.'

'What's yours?'

He frowned. 'What's my what?'

'Your wound.'

His half-smile didn't reach his eyes. 'Whoa, this is starting to get heavy. Let's see… I guess I'm a little wary of investing too much of myself in a relationship because I've been let down so many times.'

'By your father?'

'Not just my father,' Lucien said, with a flicker of pain in his gaze. 'My mother died when I was in my final year of school. Of course, it wasn't her fault or anything. She had a brain aneurysm, so it wasn't as if she could give me any warning. One day she was alive, the next she wasn't.'

'I'm so sorry,' Audrey said, thinking of the secret she was keeping about his father's health and how it might hurt him to be excluded from it. 'What did you do? Did you go and live with your father after that?'

He made a sound that was part laugh, part snort. 'No. He gave me a heap of money instead to set myself up in a flat so I could finish my year at school. He didn't even come to her funeral. He was doing a show in Europe that he didn't want to cancel. After I finished school, I went to university and lived on campus.'

Audrey hadn't realised he'd had to be so self-sufficient…but then, hadn't she too had to fend for herself more times than she could count? 'It's funny how people on the outside see us as lucky to have famous parents but they don't realise it comes with a cost. A cost no amount of money can fix.'

'So what's your wound?' Lucien asked.

Audrey wished now she hadn't started this heart-to-heart. It made her feel exposed and needy when she'd spent years trying to give him the opposite impression. 'I guess it's what we talked about the other day. I have trouble believing people want to be with me because of me or because of who my mother is.'

His eyes held her with a tender beat of understanding that made something tight in her chest soften. 'So how will you heal it? Your wound, I mean.'

Audrey couldn't hold his gaze and looked at

her mineral water instead, pretending to be fascinated by the tiny stems of bubbles in the glass. 'I guess one day I might be lucky enough to meet someone who loves me for me.'

There was a strange silence…like the collectively held breath of an audience before a crucial scene in a play.

Lucien was the first to break it but his voice sounded distinctly husky. 'I'm sure you will, Audrey.'

But it won't be you...

CHAPTER EIGHT

LUCIEN DIDN'T ALLOW his thoughts to run to what sort of man would fall in love with Audrey. Not because he didn't want her to find happiness but because he didn't want to examine too closely the strange sense of discomfort he felt at the thought of her with someone else.

Someone other than him.

Which was quite frankly ridiculous of him because he wasn't in the market for a long-term relationship. None that involved emotions like love. Never had been, never would be. Too many complications when things turned sour, as they nearly always did. He was still cleaning up the financial messes from every time his father had fallen in 'love'.

He liked his life the way it was. Dating didn't have to be complicated when you were clear about your terms. And he was always clear. Although, he had to admit, this thing he had going with Audrey was a little blurry around the edges. He couldn't just have a weekend fling and set her free. Not after sharing her first time. She was still finding her way sexually and it would be cruel to cut it short. Cruel to her and cruel to him because he had never had such intimate sex before. Sex that was intensely physical but with an added element of emotional depth he hadn't expected.

She hadn't just shared her body with him. They had both shared confidences they hadn't shared with anyone else. He'd told her more than he'd told anyone about his father—even stuff about his mother. They had talked as intimately as they had made love. No holds barred, no screens or barriers up.

No secrets.

He was surprised by her change of heart over her mother's marriage to his father. What had brought that about? Or was she tired of traipsing around the country looking for people who didn't want to be found? He was a little tired of it himself but he was sure his father was here. He couldn't explain it. He wasn't normally one for relying on gut feelings. He was a numbers and data man. But ever since he'd driven with Audrey into St Remy he'd sensed his father's presence and he wasn't going to leave until he knew one way or the other.

Lucien watched Audrey eat her chocolate *religieuse*, somehow without getting any traces of chocolate on her mouth, which was a pity because he could think of nothing better than kissing it off. And not just kissing her mouth, but every inch of her body. He was getting hard just thinking about it. Uncomfortably hard. *I-want-you-now* hard.

She suddenly looked up from her dessert and caught him watching her. She picked up her napkin and dabbed it around her mouth, her expression a little sheepish. 'I think you can see now why I don't have my mother's figure.'

He smiled. 'I like your figure just the way it

is. In fact, I'm having wicked fantasies about your figure right now.'

Her cheeks gave a delicate blush and her toffee-brown eyes twinkled like fairy lights. 'Didn't you want to go for a walk after dinner?'

It was scary how easily she could distract him from his mission, and if it hadn't been for her inexperience, he would have taken her straight back to the hotel and made love to her again and again and again.

But it wasn't just about pacing her. He had to pace himself. He was acting like a lovestruck teenager, all raging hormones and out-of-control feelings. Feelings he wouldn't allow any purchase because he wasn't going to be a fool like his father and fall in and out of love and leave a trail of despair and destruction behind. 'Walk first, bed later,' he said, softening his words with another smile.

A flicker of disappointment flashed over her features. 'Do we have to walk now? We've been on the go all day and—'

He took her hand and brought it up to his

mouth, kissing her bent fingers. 'Just a short walk, okay? That's what we're here for, remember?'

Her eyes skittered away from his. 'How could I forget? It's not like you really want to be here with me. I'm a convenient bonus bit of entertainment while you get on with your mission of breaking up your father's relationship with my mother.'

Lucien frowned at her tone and brought her gaze back to his with a finger beneath her chin. 'That was your mission too, up until today. And I'm here with you because I want to be here with you.'

Because right now I can't imagine being with anyone else.

Audrey gave him one of her cute pouts that made him want to kiss her so badly he had to glue his butt to his chair. 'Do you mean that?' Her voice came out whispery soft.

He stroked her cheek with his thumb. 'It kind of scares me how much I mean it.' It scared him even more to have admitted it out loud.

Her eyes went all shimmery as if she was close to tears but she blinked rapidly a couple of times and gave him a tight smile. 'Sorry. I know this is just a fling and I promise I won't get all clingy and start dragging my feet past jewellery shops or anything, but I just want for once in my life to be special to someone, even if it's for a short time.'

Lucien brought her hand back up to his mouth, holding her bent knuckles against his lips. 'You are special, sweetheart.' So special he was having trouble recalling his reasons for keeping his relationship with her sensibly short. 'You're amazingly special.'

'I think you're pretty special too.' She gave him a wry smile and, pulling away from him, added, 'Not special enough for me to fall in love with but special all the same.'

He didn't want her to fall in love with him, so why did her throwaway comment sting like a dart? In the past, things always got a little messy when any of his lovers had said those three little words, and these days he carefully extricated himself from the relationship well before it could happen.

But now he felt a strange sense of emptiness… a hole inside him that opened up like a painful fissure at the thought of Audrey saying those words to another man. He had never said them to anyone apart from his mother and even then he hadn't said them enough times. It was one of his biggest regrets that he hadn't told his mother how much he loved and appreciated her for all the sacrifices she had made for him. He couldn't even remember the last time he'd told her, which was even more distressing.

Audrey did her lip-chewing thing. 'I'm sorry. Have I offended you?'

Lucien quickly rearranged his frowning features into an easy-going smile. 'Why would I be offended?'

'I don't know…you were frowning so heavily, I thought I must have upset you.'

'I was thinking about my mother, actually,' Lucien said. 'I can't remember the last time I told her I loved her before she died. It's niggled at me for years.'

'I'm sure she knew it without your having to say it,' Audrey said. 'You probably showed it in heaps of ways.'

He gave her a crooked smile. 'Maybe.'

There was a little silence.

'Have you told your father you love him?' Audrey asked.

'No.' He had never felt comfortable enough within his relationship with his father to say it. He had only realised he cared about his father in the last few years, especially seeing him go through the last break-up with Sibella. It had made Lucien realise how much he cared about him when he thought he was going to lose him.

And yet he hadn't told him he loved him.

Was it anger that held him back? Anger at the reckless way his father had always lived his life? Anger at the way he had left Lucien's mother to struggle on her own as a single mum with no support? Anger that even now, when his father should be acting responsibly and sensibly, he was doing the opposite?

Audrey winced as if she found the thought of him not saying it to his father painful. 'Maybe you should…you know, before it's too late…or something…'

He let out a long sigh. 'Yeah, maybe I should.' He drummed his fingers on the table for a moment, then pushed back his chair to stand. 'Come on, little lady. Time for some fresh air before bed.'

'Can I use the bathroom first?'

'Sure. I'll settle the bill and wait for you at the front.'

Audrey dashed into the bathroom and checked her phone. The message still hadn't been read by her mother, which meant Sibella had her phone switched off. Normally her mother never switched her phone off in case her agent wanted to call her. It used to drive Audrey crazy whenever she spent time with her because her mother would always be checking her phone instead of listening to her. Why hadn't she thought to ask exactly where her mother and Harlan were staying?

She went back out to where Lucien was waiting for her at the front of the restaurant and when he smiled her heart gave a little kick. They had talked like a real couple over dinner, sharing hurts and disappointments about their lives that she—and she suspected he—had never shared with anyone else.

But they weren't a real couple. Not in the sense that this relationship—this fling—could go any significant distance. Which would have been perfectly fine even a couple of days ago because back then she hadn't seen herself wanting any relationship to go the distance, especially the distance towards marriage and happy-ever-after.

But after running into her mother and seeing the heartfelt love and distress on her face at the thought of permanently losing the love of her life Audrey had undergone a change—a change that both surprised and terrified her. She had promised not to fall in love with Lucien. She had told him it wasn't going to happen.

But hadn't it already happened?

Hadn't she already opened her heart to him both literally and figuratively? By sharing her body with him, by allowing him to be her first lover, it had made it darn near impossible not to fall in love with him. He'd been so gentle and considerate. He insisted on putting her needs ahead of his. He made her feel special. Damn it, he even told her she *was* special. He'd sounded pretty damn convincing.

Was it too much of a pipe dream to hope he might love her?

Lucien led her outside with her arm looped through one of his. The night had cooled down considerably but there were still plenty of people out and about. Audrey hoped none of them would be Harlan or her mother, but who knew what they might want to do, since this might be Harlan's last few months or even weeks of life? They might risk the threat of exposure by the press to enjoy a romantic dinner out, or a leisurely walk through the quaint village at night, when it was less easy to be recognised.

Within a block they came to the restaurant Harlan and Audrey's mother had frequented in the past. 'That's it,' Lucien said. 'It's had a name change but that's the building.' He looked through the window for any sign of his father and Sibella while Audrey's heart began a bumpy ride to her throat.

After a moment, he sighed and turned away from the window. 'No sign of them in there.'

'That's because they're in Barcelona.' Audrey hated lying to him. She felt tainted, soiled by the secret her mother had begged her to keep.

For the first time she saw a tiny flicker of doubt pass across his features. 'Maybe, maybe not.' He gave her arm a gentle pat. 'It's getting late anyway.'

They walked back to their hotel in silence. Audrey felt torn at the way she was keeping her knowledge about his father's illness from him, especially when he'd told her how gutted he'd felt when his mother died. What if something happened and he never got to say those words to his father? She opened her mouth a couple of times on the way back to the hotel but then closed it again. She had made a promise to her mother. And it was Harlan's place to deliver the news to Lucien, not hers. Not only that, but she also knew how determined Lucien was to end Harlan and Sibella's relationship. She had been just as determined a matter of days ago. What would a couple more days do? Her mother had asked—*begged*—for three days to be left alone with Harlan. One of those days was almost over. Two more to go.

'You're very quiet,' Lucien said when they got back to their room.

Audrey forced a smile to her lips. 'Just tired, I guess.'

He gathered her close, brushing her hair back from her face with a touch so gentle it made her heart contract. His eyes searched hers for a pulsing moment before they went to her mouth. 'I told myself I wasn't going to kiss you when we got back here tonight.'

A tiny ping of hurt bruised her chest. 'Why not?'

'Because I can't seem to stop at a kiss any more.' His fingertip moved over her lips like the slow sweep of a sable brush. 'You have done some serious damage to my self-control.'

Audrey leaned closer, her hips pressing against his and her arms going around his waist. 'Yeah, well, mine's not in such good shape, either.'

'That's why I didn't kiss you at the wedding three years ago.'

Audrey blinked. 'You were going to kiss me? Really?'

'Yes. But I knew if I did I might not be able to stop.' He smiled and bent down to brush her mouth with his. 'There. I'll ration myself. One kiss.'

She lifted herself up on tiptoe and pressed a soft kiss to his mouth. 'That's one apiece. Dare you to go two apiece.'

His hands moved so they were cupping her

bottom and he drew her closer so she could feel the ridge of his arousal. 'Mmm…not sure that's wise.'

'Go on,' Audrey said. 'You're not going to back down from a dare, are you?'

His eyes glinted. 'You're playing with a fire that is already burning out of control.'

She moved against him and shuddered with the same longing she could feel in his body. 'I don't want you to be in control. I want you to make love to me.'

Regret tightened his expression. 'It's too soon. You need time to—'

'I need you, Lucien,' Audrey said, holding his face in her hands. 'I need you now.'

He lowered his mouth to hers in a long, sensual kiss that made every cell in her body ache for his possession. His tongue entered her mouth in a sexy glide that mimicked the intimate entry of his body, tangling with hers in an erotic combat that made her inner core clench with need. He groaned against her mouth and his hands on her bottom gripped her even tighter against the swollen heat of his erection. 'I want you so damn much it hurts,' he said.

'I want you too,' Audrey said, planting kisses on his mouth one after the other. 'Want, want, want you.'

He led her to the bedroom, stopping every couple of steps to place another kiss on her lips. Once they were in the bedroom, Audrey kicked off her shoes and slipped out of her clothes, her gaze feasting on him as he did the same. They came back together naked, skin-on-skin, and she sighed with delight. 'If anyone had told me a couple of days ago I'd be stripping off my clothes in front of you without flinching in embarrassment I would have said they were certifiably crazy.'

Lucien gave her a teasing smile. 'Does that mean you're not going to blush any more?'

'Urgh. I hate how I blush.'

He stroked a lazy finger down the slope of her cheek. 'I think it's cute. I only have to look at you a certain way and off you go. There. You're doing it now.'

Audrey grimaced. 'That's because you're looking at me like you're going to eat me.'

His eyes glittered and he guided her towards the bed, drawing her down beside him. 'That's exactly what I'm going to do.'

Audrey shivered when his hand came down on her belly, her legs trembling at the thought of the pleasure and raw intimacy to come. He parted her first with his fingers as gently as if she were a precious hothouse orchid that needed careful handling. Then he brought his mouth to her, using his tongue to trace her, sending her senses haywire like a sudden power surge. Electric sensations flickered through her pelvis and down her thighs in little pulses and currents. He continued the sensual torture until she was tipped over the edge of a precipice, falling, falling, falling into an abyss of sublime pleasure that ricocheted through her body, making even the arches of her feet contract. 'Oh. My. God…'

Lucien moved back up her body, planting kisses on her flesh along the way: her hips, her belly, her ribcage and then her breasts, finally making it to her mouth. Tasting her essence on his mouth was so intensely erotic and it made another barrier around her heart come down like paint peeling off a wall. 'You're so sexy when you come,' he said.

Sexy. Now, that was a word she had never used to describe herself. But she felt it when she was with Lucien. She felt sexy and beautiful and… and special. She smiled and traced his mouth with her finger. 'Sexy, huh?'

He captured her finger and sucked on it deeply, releasing it to say, 'Extremely sexy.'

Audrey slipped her hand down to caress him. 'I think you're pretty sexy too.'

He drew in a deep, shuddery breath as her hand moved up and down his shaft. 'You can keep touching me like that if you like.'

'What? And not have you inside me where I want you?'

He placed a gentle hand on her belly once more, his gaze full of concern. 'The last thing I want to do is hurt you again.'

Audrey brought his head down so his mouth

was within a breath of hers. 'You worry too much. You won't hurt me.'

For a moment she thought he was going to pull away but then he gave her a lopsided smile. 'See how dangerous you are? You're making me shift all my boundaries.'

Not quite all of them.

It would be foolish to hope he would unlock his heart for her, but who said she wasn't foolish? She'd been foolish from the first moment she'd met him. But that schoolgirl crush had morphed into something far more dangerous. Dangerous because she was never going to be happy with a simple, no-strings fling. How could she have thought she would be? She wasn't built that way. She was more like her mother than she realised. She wanted marriage. She needed the security of a formal commitment.

She needed to be loved, not just lusted over.

Lucien kissed the side of her neck, his evening stubble tickling her skin and making her forget all about her reservations over their current relationship. This was what they had now—this mad lust for each other that made everything else fade into the background.

His mouth came back to hers in a deep kiss that rocked her senses like an earthquake in a glass factory. She shivered as his tongue played with hers, calling it into a seductive dance that made her toes curl with pleasure. He moved down her body, kissing and caressing her breasts, teasing the nipples into hard peaks.

He left her momentarily to reach for a condom, coming back to position himself above her, his legs in a sexy tangle with hers. 'Tell me if I'm going too fast for you.'

'You're not going fast enough,' Audrey said, lifting her hips to receive him, sighing with sheer delight when he entered her with a smooth, slick but gentle thrust. She could feel her body wrap around him, triggering pleasurable sensations in her intimate muscles.

He moved within her body, slowly at first, making sure she was comfortable until increasing his pace. If she hadn't been in love with him before, his lovemaking would have surely tipped her over. She could feel his restraint, the way he was gauging every gasp and whimper of hers, treating her with the utmost care and respect while tantalising her senses into a frenzy of delight. He stroked her intimately to give her that extra bit of friction she needed to finally fly. The orgasm swept her up in a whirlpool that made her thoughts fade to the background until she was only aware of the ripples and waves of ecstasy that were consuming her entire body. His release came soon after hers and she felt it shudder through him. He pressed against her, totally spent, his breathing heavy and uneven against her neck.

Audrey stroked his back and shoulders, content to hold him close in the blissful aftermath. But her thoughts kept drifting to the future… the future he wasn't promising to share with her. Who else would she love other than him? Who else would she want to make love with and lie like this with her body still tingling from his touch? She couldn't imagine a future without him and yet there was no future with him. Not unless he changed his mind. Not unless he fell in love with her as deeply as she had fallen in love with him.

Lucien lifted his head and gave a long, deep sigh, not quite meeting her gaze. 'I guess this was always going to feel a little different with you.' He picked up a strand of her hair and tucked it behind her ear. His eyes meshed with hers for a beat before he looked back at her mouth. 'A nice different, of course.'

'Because we already had a relationship of sorts?' Audrey screwed up her mouth and added, 'Well, hardly a relationship. An acquaintance maybe?'

He gave a wry smile and found another stray hair to tuck away. 'I guess I hadn't realised how much in common we had with our parents, acting like out-of-control teenagers all the time. Plus, I've been fighting this attraction for longer than I care to admit.'

'You're good at hiding what you're feeling. I thought you hated me.'

His crooked smile returned. 'Hate is a strong

word. I guess what I hated was the way you made me feel.'

'What did I make you feel?' The question was begging to be asked, so she asked it, even though she was worried she might be disappointed with his answer. But before he could answer there was the sound of her phone ringing from inside her bag in the other room.

'Do you want to get that?' he said.

'Whoever it is can leave a message.'

He frowned. 'What if it's your mother?'

Audrey sighed. 'You're right.' He moved aside so she could get off the bed but before she could get to the bedroom door the phone had stopped. She slipped on a bathrobe, tied the ends loosely and padded out to where her bag was. She took the phone out and saw the missed call was from her mother. She was about to press 'redial' when it started to ring again. There was no way of hiding the call from Lucien because he had followed her out of the bedroom and was standing near by. She took a breath and answered the phone. 'Hello?'

Her mother was a television star but right then her voice sounded as if it were theatre-trained. It projected out of the phone as if she were trying to reach the back row of a five-thousand-seat auditorium. 'Oh, thank God you answered. Harlan's collapsed. He had a seizure and I can't bring him round. Help me. Please help me. I don't know what to do!'

Audrey glanced at Lucien's shocked face and before she could answer he took the phone from her. 'Sibella, it's me, Lucien. Have you called an ambulance?' His brow was so tightly furrowed it looked as if it would split the bones of his skull. 'Where are you?'

Audrey swallowed a triple knot of panic. Panic for Harlan. Panic for her mother. Panic for Lucien. She listened as her mother said they were in St Remy in a farmhouse a short drive away.

'Okay, listen to me,' Lucien's voice was calm and authoritative. 'Give me the address. I'll call an ambulance. You stay with him and check his breathing and pulse. Do you know how to do CPR? Good. Try and stay calm and we'll be there as quickly as we can.'

He ended the call and used Audrey's phone to call an ambulance. She listened to him give the information in that enviably calm voice and wondered how he was ever going to forgive her if his father didn't regain consciousness.

'Get dressed,' he said as soon as he ended the call with the emergency services.

Audrey got dressed and later wondered how she'd managed to do it without putting something on back to front or inside out. Her heart was beating in her throat like a pigeon stuck in a pipe and her palms were sweaty and her legs trembling so much she could barely get them to transport her to Lucien's car.

He drove like a rally driver, only managing to remain within the designated speed limits because he wasn't the sort of man to put others' lives at risk. 'Damn it. I knew they were here,' he said, his hands gripping the steering wheel so tightly she could see the whitened bulge of his knuckles.

Should she tell him she'd known it too? She was ashamed for thinking he might not have to find out. Her mother hadn't said anything to betray her part in the secrecy. There hadn't been time with all the panic that was going on. Maybe nothing would be said. Maybe her part in the cover-up wouldn't be exposed. 'Lucien…' She moistened her bone-dry lips and tried to get her voice to cooperate past that scratchy whisper of sound.

'I *knew* she would do this to him.' He banged one of his hands on the steering wheel with such force she thought it would snap off the steering column. 'I knew she would kill him in the end. They've probably been drinking for days and God knows what else.'

She wanted to express her hurt at his misjudgement of her mother but knew it would be pointless. She sat in a miserable silence, not even able to access the words of comfort she knew she should be giving him at such a harrowing time.

He flicked her a quick glance. 'Sorry. I know

she's your mother but if I find out she's played any role in making him unwell…' He didn't finish the sentence but his jaw locked so tightly she could see a muscle working overtime.

'It's okay…'

The ambulance had already arrived by the time they found the farmhouse. Lucien rushed inside with Audrey just as they were loading his still unconscious father onto the stretcher. He went to his father's side and grasped one of his limp hands. 'Dad?'

It nearly tore Audrey's heart out of her chest to hear him say that word. She had never heard him refer to his father as anything but 'Harlan' or 'my father'.

Audrey's mother stood wringing her hands and sobbing uncontrollably. Audrey went to her and gathered her close, trying her best to comfort her but knowing it would never be enough. 'Try not to panic, Mum. They'll take good care of him. The sooner he's in hospital the better.'

Sibella pulled out of Audrey's hold. 'I need to go in the ambulance with him.'

'No,' Lucien said, stepping in the way.

Sibella straightened like a flagpole defying a hurricane. 'You can't stop me, Lucien. You're not his next of kin. I am. I'm his wife. We got married yesterday.'

CHAPTER NINE

AUDREY HAD NEVER seen anyone look more furious than Lucien at that point. But somehow he managed to control himself enough to step aside to let her mother get into the back of the ambulance. His eyes flashed like lightning when he took Audrey's hand to lead her back to his car, the grip of his hand around hers painfully tight. 'No doubt they've been celebrating ever since they tied the knot. He's probably got alcohol poisoning or something. Excessive alcohol can cause swelling on the brain. It can set off seizures.'

She closed her eyes for a brief moment, wishing she could open them again and find this was all a bad dream. 'Lucien…there's something I—'

'You know what really gets to me?' he said before she could complete her sentence. 'The way she crowed about their marriage. What was that about next of kin? I'm his only child. *I'm* his next of kin. She's just another one of the wives he's loved and who's left him.'

Audrey drew in a breath that clawed at her throat like a fishhook. 'She *is* his legal next of kin, Lucien. That's the whole point of marrying someone you love—so they can be with you at all the important stages of your life. He wanted to marry her and he did. You shouldn't be questioning it. You have to accept it. They love each other and want to spend any time that's remaining with each other.'

She felt his glance like the thrust of a dagger. The silence building in tension, stretching, stretching, stretching like an elastic band pulled too tight.

'You knew they were here.' He thumped the steering wheel again, his breath leaving his mouth in a rush. 'You knew they were here, didn't you?'

Audrey couldn't look at him and looked instead at her hands in her lap. 'I've been trying to tell you—'

'When did you find out?' His voice was so hard she was surprised it didn't shatter the window on her side of the car.

'Today.'

'Today?' She could almost hear the cogs of his brain ticking over. 'Before or after we had sex?'

Audrey put a hand to her forehead. 'Don't do this, Lucien. Please. Isn't everyone upset enough without—?'

'You've taken prostitution to a whole new level.' The words were as savage as lethal arrows. 'You saw your mother at the market, didn't you? You saw her and then lied to me. You lied to me and then offered yourself like some sort of boudoir distraction to stop me from continuing the search.'

She swallowed without speaking, unable to look at him, unable to witness the caustic loathing and hatred she could hear in his words.

'Answer me, damn it!'

Audrey flinched and fought back tears. 'I made a promise—'

'A promise?' Scorn dripped from his tone like corrosive acid.

'I ran into my mother at the market and she begged me not to tell you that your father was unwell with a brain tumour,' Audrey said. 'She wanted to talk him into having surgery. He was refusing all treatment and she was trying to talk him round. She loves him, Lucien, and he loves her. They want to be together with whatever time is remaining. They were both worried you would try and talk them out of being together. I agreed to keep their location a secret because… because I wish someone loved me like that.'

Her words dropped into a cavernous silence.

'Let me get this straight…you've known since earlier today that my father was critically unwell and you didn't see it as a priority to inform me of that fact?'

How could she explain her motivations when he put it like that? How could she tell Lucien his father hadn't wanted him to know about his illness until after he was married to her mother? It seemed too cruel to dump that on him now when he was already so upset. 'I made a promise to my—'

'I don't care what promise you made to your mother,' he said. 'This is about my father, not your mother. I had the right to know he was unwell.'

'I know… I'm sorry. I should have told you but I didn't want to hurt her. She trusted me and I wanted to honour that trust.'

'And what about the trust that had developed between us?' His eyes bored into hers, as determined as a drill through steel. 'Didn't that count for something?'

'We're having a fling, Lucien. It's not the same as a committed or formal relationship.'

He pulled into the hospital entrance with a squeal of brakes. He parked the car before he spoke, his hand still gripping the steering wheel with white-knuckled force. He didn't turn to look at her but stared fixedly straight ahead. 'Would you have entered into a fling with me if you hadn't run into your mother today?' His voice was so cold it made her skin shiver.

'Yes. Yes, I would.'

His glance was so pointed she felt as if she'd been jabbed with a pin. 'Sorry but I don't believe you. You offered yourself to me because you knew it would be enough of a distraction to stop me trawling the streets of the village.'

She took a breath and continued. 'That's not true. I wanted to make love with you. I settled for a fling but I think we could have more than that, Lucien. I think you know that too. We're good together—you said it yourself. You said how different it was between us than your other—'

'Oh, you thought this was going to *go* somewhere?' The derision in his tone was as savage as a switchblade. 'So you lied to me about that too. You told me you never wanted to get married. But all the time you've been hanging out for the fairy tale. Well, guess what? It's over. I'm ending it right here, right now. I should have trusted my instincts and left you well alone.'

Audrey had been preparing herself for this moment but now that it had come it was even more devastating than she'd thought. He was upset, of course he was, and he had every right to be. She would be too if the situation was reversed. He needed time to come to terms with the shock of his father's illness. Maybe he would change his mind once he talked to his father… her stomach swooped…*if* he ever got the chance to talk to his father. 'Can we talk about this later, when you've had time to—?'

'Did you hear me?' His voice contained an edge of steel that made every hair on her head shiver at the roots. 'I said it's over.'

Audrey couldn't look at him and quietly gathered her bag from the floor. 'I'm just going to see my mother and then I'll get a cab back to the hotel to collect my things. I'll stay with her until the…the crisis is over with your father.'

'Fine.'

Fine? Was that all he could say after what they'd shared? Nothing was fine about this. Audrey's heart felt like it was jammed between two solid, splinter-ridden planks, every breath she took increasing the pressure. Her eyes stung with tears but she refused to cry in front of him. She couldn't bear the humiliation of him witnessing her heartbreak.

She followed him into the hospital but he barely gave her a glance. He went straight to the desk to ask where his father had been taken and Audrey peeled away to find her mother.

She was in the waiting room outside the emergency room and Audrey went straight to her and enveloped her in a hug. 'Oh, Mum, I'm so sorry. Is there any news?'

Sibella lifted her tear-stained face off Audrey's shoulder, her bottom lip trembling. 'They're going to do a CAT scan to see what's going on. They think he's having some sort of intracranial bleed from the tumour. They're going to fly him to Paris for surgery because they don't have the facilities here. I can't bear the thought of losing him. Not now that I've finally got him back.'

'I know, it's so sad,' Audrey said, blinking back her own tears. 'But you've been with him for the last few days and made him as happy as you could. Hold on to that.'

'We had such a lovely wedding ceremony,' Sibella said, taking the tissue Audrey handed her and mopping at her eyes. 'So intimate and private at the farmhouse in the garden. I'm sorry I didn't invite you and Lucien but Harlan wanted it to be just us this time. No fanfare. No fuss. Just us.'

'I think you did the right thing,' Audrey said. 'I'm glad you two got married again. I couldn't be happier for you. Well, I could if Harlan wasn't so unwell.'

Her mother looked at her with reddened eyes. 'You really mean that, don't you?'

Audrey smiled. 'Perhaps you and Harlan do belong together. You're lucky to have experienced such passionate love not once but three times. I hope and pray he gets through this so you can prove all the doubters wrong.'

'Speaking of doubters,' Sibella said, glancing past Audrey for any sign of Lucien, 'I hope I haven't made things difficult between you and Lucien.'

Audrey wasn't going to burden her mother with her own heartbreak at this point, if ever. Sibella had enough emotion to deal with without Audrey dumping more on her. 'No, it's fine. He's upset about his father, of course. It's been a terrible shock for him.'

Her mother's gaze searched hers. 'You're not in love with him or anything, are you?'

'In love?' Audrey made an attempt at a laugh but it sounded more like a choke. 'We had a bit of a fling but we've called time on it. It was never going to work. I'm not his type and he's not mine.'

Sibella chewed at her lower lip for a moment, her brow creased in a tiny frown. 'It's not always about being the right type of person, sweetie. It's about the right type of love you feel for each other. It took me three times to find that love with Harlan but now I've found it I'm going to hold on to it no matter what.'

'Lucien doesn't love me, Mum,' Audrey said

in a quiet voice. 'I don't think he's capable of loving anyone like that.'

'Mrs Fox?' A doctor with an English accent came towards them and stopped in front of Sibella. 'The air patient transfer has been arranged so we're taking your husband soon. He's not conscious but if you'd like to spend a couple of minutes with him before the flight to Paris that would be okay.'

'Oh, thank you,' Sibella said and followed the doctor away to where Harlan was being held.

Audrey sighed and went back to the waiting room to wait for her mother to return, wondering if it would have been wiser to leave now before there was any chance of running into Lucien. Had he had a chance to spend time with his father?

Lucien walked out of the hospital after speaking to his father's doctor and stood for a moment trying to get his emotions under control. His father had cancer. A brain tumour. It was operable but the risks of permanent damage were huge. His fun-loving, irresponsible and reckless father might turn into a comatose body on a ventilator. He couldn't understand why his father hadn't told him he was ill. He handled all his father's financial affairs, fixed up every mess and monitored every detail of his father's life and yet his father had shut him out of this health crisis. What sort of father did that to his only son? Didn't his father realise how much he cared about him?

But it was Audrey's role in the cover-up that was eating at him the most. She had only slept with him to distract him from finding out where his father and Sibella were. He'd thought…he'd thought… Damn it. He wasn't going to think about it now. He wasn't going to think their relationship was different from anything he'd experienced before because it wasn't different. It was just a fling that had turned sour. But it had only turned sour because she'd deceived him. Openly lied to his face, making him believe…

No. No. No. Don't go there.

He had to stop thinking she might have been

The One. The one person—the only person—he could see himself building a future with that involved trust and openness and, yes, even love. But it was all a bald-faced lie. Their relationship had sprung up out of her desperation to keep him from the truth about his father's and her mother's whereabouts.

Had she been working against him from the start?

He mentally backtracked through the last couple of days, wondering how he could have been so stupid to be hoodwinked by lust. That was all it was, of course. Lust. He refused to consider it as anything else. He'd lusted after her and she'd seen it as an opportunity to manipulate him. Now his father was dying and his next of kin was that attention-seeking, wine-swilling witch Sibella, who gloated over his father's unconscious body about her brand-new status as his wife.

For the third freaking time.

Lucien dragged in a lungful of cool night air, trying to loosen the tight feeling in his chest. It might be hours before his father came out of surgery in Paris. It might be hours, days even, before there was news, either good or bad. He didn't want to see Audrey. He never wanted to see her again. Seeing her would remind him of every cunning and clever lie she'd told him and how he'd foolishly fallen for it.

Fallen for her.

No. Damn it. No. He'd fallen in lust. He wasn't going to name it as anything else. What was the point in admitting she had done what no other woman had done? What he had allowed no other woman to do. He had lost his head over her. Lost everything he had worked so hard to maintain. Her betrayal had stung him, more than stung him, but it was the fact she had got into his heart that hurt the most. He should never have allowed it to happen. He should have taken greater care. He should have resisted her.

Lust, not love. Lust, not love. Lust, not love. If he had to say it like a mantra until he believed it then that was what he would damn well do.

Lust was all it was and now it was over.

CHAPTER TEN

AUDREY HADN'T BOTHERED collecting her things from the hotel and had flown with her mother to Paris as soon as she could organise a flight. By the time they arrived at the large and busy Paris hospital, Harlan was still on a ventilator but the bleed had been controlled and a large section of the tumour had been removed. The neurosurgeon had expressed cautious optimism that Harlan would regain consciousness in a few days when the swelling had receded.

Audrey had been terrified of running into Lucien when she and her mother came to the hospital, but, given the size of the place, somehow she had managed to miss him and hadn't seen him since the night they'd followed the ambulance to the smaller hospital in St Remy.

The time spent supporting her mother was just

the distraction she needed to take her mind off her own heartache. But in spite of the warm and loving chats with her mother, the visits to the hospital and the day-to-day duties she assigned herself at the small Airbnb they were staying in, Audrey still had plenty of time to feel the stinging pain of Lucien's rejection. How different would this time be if he'd allowed her to support him as well as her mother?

How different would it be if he loved her as she loved him?

Audrey wanted what her mother had with Harlan this third time around. The right type of love. A mature and lasting love. A love that wanted the best for the other partner—a love that gave sacrificially instead of selfishly taking.

But Lucien had locked his heart away and built an impenetrable fortress around it. It pained her to think he thought so badly of her after all they'd shared. But he had refused to listen to her explanation and had cut her coldly and clinically and cruelly from his life.

On day five Harlan woke when his doctors

removed him from the ventilator. The first person he asked for was Sibella and Audrey sat outside ICU while her mother was taken in to see him. She couldn't help thinking how special it must be to be the first person a desperately ill patient asked for when they woke from a coma. Would she ever be that special person to someone? Would anyone love her the way Harlan loved her mother? Or would she always be lonely like this? Sitting alone in the waiting room of life.

When her mother came out a short time later she was crying but with happy tears. 'Oh, sweetie, he's awake and even managed to make a joke. He's still not out of danger but the doctors think he might be well enough for chemo in a week or two, if we can convince him to go through it.'

Audrey hugged her mother so tightly she worried she might snap a rib. 'I'm so glad he's made it this far. So very glad.'

Sibella pulled back from the hug but still held

on to Audrey's arms. 'He's asking for Lucien. Do you think you could call him? I'm not sure he'll take a call from me.'

Or from me.

Audrey took out her phone and pulled up his number. Even seeing his name there on her screen made her heart clench and her stomach sink. She pressed 'dial' and held the phone to her ear but it went straight to his message service. She tried to think of something to say but her mouth wouldn't cooperate. In the end she hung up the phone and sighed and faced her mother. 'No answer.'

'I suppose the hospital will call him,' Sibella said and scraped a hand through her blonde tresses. 'I could do with a drink.' She grinned cheekily at Audrey's frown. 'Coffee, okay? Harlan and I are booked in to do couple's rehab. I reckon we'll have more chance of kicking the habit better together than doing it alone.'

Audrey smiled and linked her arm through her mother's. 'Coffee sounds great.'

* * *

Lucien sat by his father's bedside in ICU later that day when he'd flown back in from London. He'd had some work to see to for a client awaiting his report for court so he hadn't had any choice but to fly back to London and sort it out. His father had been sleeping on and off but had woken a couple of times to speak to him. It was strange having that time with his father. Alone time, if you could call it that when you were surrounded by machines and monitors and multiple medical staff milling about as they attended to their duties.

Whenever he'd spent time with his father in the past there were always managers or publicists or other band members about. When he'd met his father for the first time when he was ten years old there'd been twenty other people in the room.

But now it felt as if it was just the two of them. A father and his son just…hanging out.

Harlan opened his eyes again and gave Lucien

a lopsided smile. 'I thought you'd have something better to do than hang around here.'

'Nowhere I'd rather be right now.'

Harlan's eyes watered. 'I haven't been a good father to you, Lucien. Thing is… I didn't know how to be a dad. Mine was a mean, sadistic bastard who beat my mother up and sold our belongings to feed his gambling habit. Beat me up too. Heaps of times.' His fingers gripped the sheet under his hand as if he was remembering each and every blow of his father's fists. 'It made me worried I might do the same…you know…if I got too close to you.'

Lucien had never heard his father mention his own father. He'd had no idea his dad's childhood had been so grim. Was that why his dad drank and partied to cover up his pain at how he'd been treated? He took his dad's hand, suddenly realising it was the first time he had ever touched him in such an affectionate way. 'You're a better father than I am a son. I've been too critical of you, too judgemental. I haven't taken the time to see the man behind the fame.'

Harlan squeezed Lucien's hand. 'I know you don't care for Sibella but I love her and want to spend whatever time I have left with her. We've been bad for each other in the past but we've made some changes. Good changes. Tough changes. I hope one day you get to feel the same sort of love for someone. Don't settle for anything less. Promise me that.'

Lucien was finding it hard to find his voice. He had already found that sort of love. What he felt for Audrey was so much more than lust. If it had been simply lust then why was he still feeling so empty? Why was he feeling like his heart had been severed from his chest? He'd been pushing his feelings from his mind. Shoving them back like a shirt in his wardrobe he couldn't bring himself to look at for the memories it triggered. He hadn't been able to stop thinking about her. Torn between dreading running into her at the hospital and yet feeling bitterly, achingly disappointed when he didn't. Tempted to call her so much he'd turned off his phone. He'd pushed her away because he'd believed she had disappointed him, betrayed him. Lied to him.

But who was the bigger liar?

He was. He'd been lying to himself for years. Six years. It had started when Audrey flirted with him at his dad's first wedding to her mother. And he'd continued lying to himself when Audrey approached him the second time, smiling up at him with those big brown eyes of hers.

And what had he done? Each time he'd pushed her away. Cruelly rejected her. She'd given herself to him. He was her first and only lover. Didn't that mean something?

His gut clenched, his heart gave a spasm and regret tasted like bile in his mouth.

It meant he'd made a terrible mistake.

Lucien brought himself back to his conversation with his father with an effort. 'Why didn't you tell me you were ill? I could have organised the best medical—'

'I made Sibella promise not to tell you,' Harlan said. 'I wanted her to know first, and then, when we got the wedding out of the way, we were going to tell you and Audrey. I didn't want either of you to try and talk us out of it. You know what you two are like. Fricking fun police, the pair of you.'

Lucien swallowed again. 'So when did Audrey find out you were ill?'

'When she ran into Sibella the other day,' Harlan said. 'She made Audrey promise not to tell you because that's what I wanted. I insisted on telling you in person but only when I was ready to. She was only acting on my wishes, Lucien. Please don't be too offended I didn't tell you first. But you have to understand Sibella's my go-to person now. The person I want to tell everything to, the good stuff and the bad stuff. It doesn't mean I don't love you. I do in my own inept and clumsy way.'

Lucien put his other hand on top of his father's and somehow managed a smile. 'I love you, too… Dad.'

Harlan blinked away tears but he was still wearing his bad-boy rock star smile. 'If you tell anyone I've been bawling like a teething baby I'll have to kill you, okay?'

* * *

Lucien walked out of ICU a short time later in a daze. What had he done? He'd destroyed his only chance at happiness with Audrey. He'd ruthlessly, cruelly cut her from his life. He hadn't given her time to explain anything. If only he'd listened. If only he'd realised his feelings for her weren't a bad thing. She was the best thing that had ever happened to him. Just like Sibella was for his father. The love Sibella and his father shared had matured into something that could withstand illness, even death.

It was exactly the sort of love he felt for Audrey. He had fought so hard not to fall for her. He had fought so hard not to lose control. But she had been too much for his willpower. She had always been too much for his willpower, which was why he'd held her aloft for so long.

His chest cramped as if someone had kicked him square in the heart. What if he'd lost her? Was it too late to tell her? Was it too late to hope she might forgive him? Sweat prickled his back and shoulders. A sick feeling churned in his stomach. He couldn't lose her. Not now. Not now he'd finally realised he'd been waiting for this sort of love for most of his adult life.

He couldn't lose her.

Oh, God. If he lost her…

Audrey left her mother chatting to some fans in the hospital cafeteria. The press had been around when they'd first arrived at the hospital but she had managed to avoid them. Sibella had issued a press release about Harlan's condition and asked for privacy and, thankfully, that was mostly what they'd had. Now that Harlan was a little better, Audrey knew it would soon be time for her to go back to London. She knew she should have already made arrangements well before now but hadn't been able to let go of a gossamer thread of hope Lucien might seek her out and tell her he'd changed his mind.

She was walking along the wide corridor when she saw him walking towards her. She considered darting into one of the storage rooms out of sight, but his stride length increased and so did his speed. Before she could make up her mind which door to choose he was within arm's reach. 'Audrey?' The way he said her name made her heart skip. Was that a note of…of desperation in his voice?

She kept her face blank and turned with her spine so rigid and straight it looked as if she'd just graduated as star pupil from deportment school. 'Yes?'

His expression was hard to read but she thought she could see a flicker of worry in his eyes. 'I need to talk to you.'

'I think you've said all that needs to be—'

He held her by the upper arms, his voice gruff and with that same note of desperation she'd heard before. 'Please, sweetheart. Just hear me out. I know I don't deserve it after the way I cut you from my life the other day. I was wrong to blame you for not telling me about my father's illness. You were acting on his wishes and I would've done exactly the same if the tables were turned.'

Audrey wasn't ready to forgive him. Why

should she when he'd treated her so cruelly? He could apologise all he liked but it wasn't an apology she wanted from him. She wanted his love and that was unlikely to be why he was standing in front of her now. He was too proud a man to grovel. He was probably clearing his conscience after his cosy little chat with his father. 'Oh, so now you're apologising because he's told you he was the one who insisted you not be told? How terribly gallant of you, Lucien.'

He gave a slow blink as if her words pained him like a vicious stab but he still maintained his hold on her arms. 'I'd already realised I loved you before my father told me he'd insisted I not be told.' His hands slid down her arms to grasp her hands, holding them gently. 'I love you, Audrey. I think I've been in love with you ever since you hit on me at our parents' first wedding.'

Audrey couldn't find her voice. She opened and closed her mouth and blinked a couple of times to make sure she wasn't imagining this conversation. 'You…you love me? Really and truly love me?'

He smiled a wide smile that made his dark blue eyes shine. 'Really and truly and desperately love you. I've been such a fool for denying it all this time. I don't know why I did. It's so obvious you're the only one for me. You're the other half of my heart. I feel so empty without you. Will you marry me, sweetheart?'

Audrey beamed up at him and threw her arms around his neck. 'You're the only person I want to marry. I love you. I don't want anyone else but you. I think that's why I never dated all these years because I've been secretly waiting for you.'

'The wait is over, my darling,' Lucien said, holding her close. 'We belong together. I can't imagine how miserable my life would be without you in it.'

'I was so sad when you ended our fling—'

'Don't call it that ever again.' He grimaced as if in pain. 'It was never a fling. It was never just about lust, even though I kept telling myself it was. It was always about love. How could I have been so deluded as to convince myself otherwise?'

'I did it too,' Audrey said, holding on to him to keep herself from falling over out of sheer relief and joy. 'I pretended I hated you. I couldn't even hear your name mentioned without wanting to grind my teeth to powder. But I was always a bit in love with you.'

He grimaced again. 'I can't bear to think we might have missed out on being together. I've been such an idiot. Forgive me? Please?'

'Of course I forgive you. I love you.'

He brushed her hair back from her face. 'I want to build a life together. Do you want children? God, I can't believe I'm even asking that in a hospital corridor.'

'Do you want them?'

'I asked first.'

Audrey gazed into his twinkling eyes. 'I only want them if they're yours.'

He smiled and brought his mouth down to hers. 'I'll see what I can do.'

EPILOGUE

Ten months later...

LUCIEN SAT NEXT to Audrey at the dining table at Bramble Cottage. She reached for his hand under the table and, smiling at him, gave it a squeeze. His heart gave a leap just as it always did when her beautiful brown eyes looked at him like that. He smiled back and winked at her and, yes, she still blushed.

'Hey, you two, the honeymoon should be well and truly over by now,' Harlan said, from the other side of the table. His hair hadn't grown back yet from the gruelling chemo but his cranial scar was fading and his specialists were happy with his progress so far. So far. No promises were being made about a complete recovery but Lucien was determined that, no matter what awaited them in the weeks and months ahead, his father's happiness would be a top priority.

And no one made his dad happier than Sibella.

'Like you can talk,' Lucien said, smiling at the way his father's arm was around Sibella's shoulders and how she was beaming at Harlan with such love in her eyes it made him feel ashamed of how he had misjudged her in the past. His father and Sibella weren't perfect, but he had come to a place where he accepted them as they were and didn't expect them to change to suit him.

'Mum, Dad, we have something to tell you,' Audrey said, looking like she was about to burst with the secret she'd been keeping for the last couple of weeks until they hit the twelve-week mark in their pregnancy.

It just about made Lucien's heart explode with emotion every time she called his father 'Dad'. It spoke of the deep affection she had for his father, and her care and concern and nursing abilities over the last few months had made Lucien, and of course his father, love her all the more.

And now Lucien was to become a father. In

the not so distant future a little person would look up at him and call him Dad.

'Will you tell them or will I?' Audrey said, smiling at him.

He took her hand and brought it up to his mouth. 'Let's do it together.'

And so they did.

* * * * *